The Crank Case

Volume 8 of
The Casebooks
Of Octavius Bear

Harry DeMaio

"Alternative Universe Mysteries for Adult Animal
Lovers"

Paperback ISBN 978-1-78705-326-7
ePub ISBN 978-1-78705-327-4
PDF ISBN 978-1-78705-328-1

Published in the UK by MX Publishing
335 Princess Park Manor, Royal Drive,
London, N11 3GX
www.mxpublishing.co.uk

Cover layout and construction by
Brian Belanger

Dedicated to GTP

A Most Extraordinary Bear

Acknowledgements

These books have evolved over a long period of time and under a wide range of influences and circumstances. I am indebted to many people for helping to bring Octavius and his cohorts to the printed page. Thanks most especially to my wife, Virginia, for her insights and clever suggestions as well as her unfailing enthusiasm for the project and patience with its author. To my sons, Mark and Andrew and their spouses, Cindy and Lorraine, for helping make these tomes more readable and audience friendly. To Cathy Hartnett, cheerleader-extraordinaire for her eagerness to see this alternate universe take form. To Jack Magan, Paul Bernish, Dan Andriacco, Amy Thomas, Luke Benjamin Kuhns and Zohreh Zand for their enthusiastic encouragement.

Kudos to Jim Effler, the late Bob Gibson and Brian Belanger for their wonderful illustrations and covers. Thanks, of course, to Steve Emecz and Timi at MX Publishing for giving Octavius et al. a great home

If, in spite of all this support, some errors or inconsistencies have crept through, the buck stops here. Needless to say, all of the characters, situations, and narratives are fictional.

Also from Harry DeMaio

1-The Open and Shut Case   2-The Case of the Spotted Band   3-The Case of Scotch   4-The Lower Case   5-The Curse of the Mummy's Case 6- The Attaché Case   7-The Suit Case

The Development of Civilization Volume Eight - Part One

Our Origins

(From "An Introduction to Faunapology" by Octavius Bear Ph.D.)

About 100,000 years ago, according to scientific experts, a colossal solar flare blasted out from our Sun, creating gigantic magnetic storms. here on Earth. These highly charged electrical tempests caused startling physical and psychological imbalances in the then population of our world. The complete nervous systems of some species were totally destroyed. For example, "Homo Sapiens" lost all mental and motor capabilities and rapidly became extinct. Less developed species exposed to the radiation were affected differently. Four-footed and finned mammals, birds and reptiles suddenly found themselves capable of complex thought, enhanced emotions, self-awareness, social consciousness and the ability to communicate, sometimes orally, sometimes telepathically, often both. Both speech production and speech perception slowly progressed with the evolution of tongues, lips, vocal cords and enhanced ear to brain connections. Many species developed opposable digits, fingers or claws, further accelerating civilized progress. Some others (most fish and underground dwellers) were shielded from the radiation and remained only as sentient as they were before the blast. This event is referred to as The Big Shock. It remains under intensive study.

The Players

- **Octavius Bear** – Mega-sized Kodiak; Narcoleptic war hero; Consulting Detective; Scientist; Inventor; Seeker of justice; Gazillionaire owner of Universal Ursine Industries; Gourmet/Gourmand; Bee Keeper; Somewhat sedentary and grouchy just on general principles.

- **Mauritius (Maury) Meerkat** – Narrator; Assistant to Octavius; Theatrical Agent; African *émigré* with a French-Dutch background; clever with a shady history.

- **Bearoness Belinda Béarnaise Bruin Bear** *(nee Black)* – Gorgeous polar superstar, with the Aquashow, *"Some Like It Cold;"* Wife of Octavius; Extremely rich widow of Bearon Byron Bruin living in Polar Paradise in the Shetlands; Owner-pilot of the last flying Concorde SST

- **Arabella Bear** – Hybrid bear cub prodigy; Twin daughter of Bearoness Belinda and Octavius.

- **McTavish Bear** – Hybrid bear cub prodigy; Twin son of Bearoness Belinda and Octavius.

- **Mlle Woof** – Bichon Frisé – Governess to the twin cubs.

- **Frau Schuylkill** – Octavius' beautiful Swiss she-wolf estate manager/cook/pilot/security officer with many other mysterious and military talents. She rescued Octavius from his dive off the Breakurbach Falls while he was struggling with his nemesis, Imperius Drake.

- **Wyatt Where** – Another wolf; Former military intelligence officer who had retired to a security post at the Bank of Lake Michigan in Chicago and then quit to join Octavius.

- **Howard Watt** – Porcupine; High tech security authority who also left the Bank to join Octavius; Alternate Universe specialist; Laser and particle beam accelerator expert.

- **Otto the Magnificent – aka Hairy Otter** – An absolutely terrible illusionist magician, Otto the Magnificent escaped the claws of super villain Imperius Drake but not before he developed some amazing powers courtesy of Imperius' genetic alterations.

- **Benedict and Galatea Tigris** – White Bengals; The Flying Tigers; Pilots of Belinda's and Octavius' aircraft; brother and sister.

- **Chief Inspector Bruce Wallaroo** – Irrepressible but brilliant marsupial; an international law and order genius from Down Under; often calls on Octavius and Maury for support.

- **Chita** – Beautiful, fascinating, clever, sexy, immoral and highly independent feline who among other things, is the publisher and editor-in-chief of *PURR* and *SOW* magazines.

- **L. Condor** – Andean Condor; cyber-net genius with a twelve-foot wingspan and artificial voice.

- **Marlin** – Dolphin (sic) the Prince of Whales' Chief Scientist, Magician and part time Jester. On-Loan partner of Howard Watt

- **Bearon Byron Bear** – Deceased husband of Bearoness Belinda.

- **Bearyl and Bearnice Blanc** – Belinda's stunning twin polar sidekicks; Actress and singer, respectively; Former co-pilot and flight engineer of Belinda's SST.

- **Leperello** – Himalayan Snow Leopard and singing partner of Bearnice Blanc. "Lepi"

- **Dougal** – Shetland Sheep Dog – Estate Manager of Bearmoral Castle / Polar Paradise.

- **Ms. Fairbearn** – Canadian Polar – Chief Housekeeper of Bearmoral Castle / Polar Paradise.
- **Bearmoral Shetland Sheep:**
  Dolly, Holly, Molly and Polly – Housemaids and probable clones.
- **Mrs. McRadish** – Sheep – Chief Cook at Polar Paradise.
- **Ian** – Red Deer – Chief of the Castle's Theatrical Stage Crew.
- **Fiona** – Dandie Dinmont Terrier – Lounge Manager at Polar Paradise.
- **Lion and Unicorn** – Proprietors of the Baltasound pub of the same name.
- **Harold** – Sea Otter in charge of the castle's beaches, pools and watercraft.
- **Superintendent Nigel Wardlaw of Shetland Yard** – Bearded Collie – The Scottish Police.
- **Jack DeLad** – Grizzly Villain.
- **Wolford Wolverine Esq.** – Octavius' lawyer and UUI's chief counsel.
- **Brittany** – Ursine Movie Ingenue.
- **Algernon Maritimus Ursine** – Polar bear from Canada.
- **Preston Pavel Polar** – Ursine Movie Star – Cousin of Paul and Paula.
- **Paul and Paula Polar** – Stunt Doubles for Preston and Brittany – Mated pair.
- **Jock and Trevor** – Terriers – Bagpipers and Oil Rig Saboteurs.
- **General Turmoil** – Horse; Leader of The Business; Intent on Cosmic Conquest.
- **Fetlock Holmes** – The Great Horse Detective and sometime associate of Octavius Bear.
- **Ursula 7** – Universal Ursine Intellect Model 7 – Artificial General Intelligence System.

Locations

Cincinnati, Ohio; UUI, Kentucky; Polar Paradise in the Shetlands, and Alternate Universes

Octavius

Prologue

Do Bears give you a scare? Well, me too.

So, I'll pass on this tactic to you.

You just fix that old Bear

With a cold, piercing stare.

But make sure that he's Winnie-the-Pooh.

As the Aquabear Concorde pointed its "droop snoot" toward the active runway at Dyce- Abeardeen Airport in Scotland, Octavius Bear awoke from his narcolepsy-induced snooze, yawned and scared the hell out of some of the other passengers. Those of us who were used to his voyages into Dream Land still jumped at the unexpected roar. This was a different sort of sonic boom.

His consort, The Bearoness Belinda Béarnaise Bruin Bear (nee Black) was at the controls of the last flying SST along with Benedict and Galatea Tigris, The Flying Tigers, who were acting as co-pilot and flight engineer. The Bearoness *(Bel to her friends and relations)* is a highly accomplished pilot of both fixed wing and rotary aircraft. Between her and Octavius, they own an impressive fleet of flying machines, housed in the Shetlands and the Bear's Lair in far off Cincinnati.

Today, our group is making yet another pilgrimage to Polar Paradise, Belinda's Shetlands residence/resort to, among other things, celebrate Christmas. To retain her Bearonial status, Bel must occupy the castle at least six months of the year. She and Octavius do a supersonic commute between their opulent homes accompanied by their twin Cubs, Arabella and McTavish and their governess, Mlle Woof. Much more of them, later.

My name is Maury *(Mauritius)* Meerkat - also known as Offscreen Narrator. When I am part of the action, I am Octavius' trusted associate and field captain. I am two feet tall plus tail and I weigh in at twenty-four pounds. He, on the other hand, is a huge Kodiak – over nine feet tall and 1400 pounds – and like many of his species is given to emotional outbursts.

As you may also know, Octavius, among his many talents and accomplishments, is a brilliant, self-taught practitioner in the wide-ranging fields of biology, physics, ursinology, voodoo, teleology, psychology, chemistry, apiculture and oenology. He is a self-made gazillionaire and sole owner of UUI *(Universal Ursine Industries.)* He is also a first rate electrical, electronic, structural, marine, computer science, aeronautical, civil, mechanical and chemical engineer. He has a few other interesting characteristics such as falling into brief, deep narcoleptic comas – side effects of his successful genetic experiments to eliminate the need for him to hibernate.

However, the talent and occupation that should interest you most is his avocation for criminology. The Bear works in close concert with Inspector Bruce Wallaroo from Australia, of whom more later, and with his own Cincinnati based team:

- Frau Ilse Schuylkill – Swiss she-wolf; Bear's Lair estate manager; Cordon Bleu chef; jet pilot and sharpshooter with other very strange and arcane abilities.

- Colonel Wyatt Where – another wolf; ex-military hero; security specialist and pilot; Frau Schuylkill's equally bizarre running mate.

- Doctor Howard Watt – porcupine; brilliant scientist and technologist; laser and weapons specialist; Multiverse expert.

- Hairy Otter aka Otto the Magnificent - An absolutely terrible illusionist magician, Otto the Magnificent escaped the claws of super villain Imperius Drake but not before he developed some amazing powers courtesy of Imperius' genetic alterations.

  - L. Condor – Andean Condor; cyber-net genius with a twelve-foot wingspan and artificial voice.

  - Ursula – Universal Ursine Intellect Model 7 – Artificial General Intelligence System.

  - Your humble servant – African Meerkat; Octavius' indispensable assistant; operative; scribe; overall facilitator; talent agent as well as a pretty clever detective, if I do say so myself.

When we are not out scouring the world for evildoers, in cooperation with local, national and international constabularies, we are headquartered in a rambling old mansion near Cincinnati which encompasses not only the Great Bear's opulent digs, but his massive laboratories and shops; his missile silo disguised as an Asian pagoda; *(don't ask)* and a large Roman temple that serves as a hangar for his four airplanes, a Twin Otter; a F15E Strike Eagle; a V-22 Osprey; a C5A-The Ursa Major; plus an AgustaWestland AW101 VVIP luxury helicopter -The Ursa Minor.

We are wrapping up our transoceanic run to the Shetlands aboard the Bearoness' SST and will soon be transferring to her shuttle helicopters for the final leg to Polar Paradise. Once a formidable castle owned by her late husband, Bearon Byron Bruin, Bel has reconverted it back to its original status as a beachfront hotel and resort. We Ohioans will be visiting for two weeks *(a fortnight)* while Bel will be staying on with her offspring and their governess for several months.

It is December, the busiest period at the castle, with polar bears from the Bearents Sea and Canada descending en masse for year-end celebrations. The Bearoness must play the role of gracious hostess and perform with the Aquabears Revue of which she is the premiere aqueuse. Otto is also a star attraction.

Touchdown accompanied by the noisy applause of the Cubs! Next, on to the whirlybirds and off to the North. Two large utility helicopters in blue and white Bearonial livery were standing next to the hangar the Bearoness keeps at the airport. Dyce is the world's busiest helicopter aerodrome, with ships servicing the North Sea Oil rigs, transferring equipment, supplies and wildcats to and from the platforms. As the Aquabear taxied up to the hangar, the Cubs were out of their seats and rushing toward the doors. Mlle Woof got in the aisle and by sheer force of personality got them seated and belted in again. Amazing how this little dog can haul in those two manic Furballs.

After securing the SST, The Flying Tigers will join us in the second chopper. Ben and Galatea will be celebrating the holidays with the rest of us. The staff at Polar Paradise still wasn't sure what to make of these very rare white felines.

Bearoness Belinda
Béarnaise Bruin
(nee Black)

Chapter One

To whom do we have to give thanks

For a nasty assortment of pranks?

They're just acting like pests.

Are they Christmas-tide guests?

Or a different collection of Cranks?

It took two choppers piloted by Belinda and the Flying Tigers to accommodate our group and our sizeable pile of baggage. *(Including Christmas presents for the Cubs.)* So far, an uneventful journey. We landed at the castle in a light snowfall further stirred up by the rotors of the two helicopters. On alighting, the Cubs jumped from their seats, pushed open the door, bounced down the skids and began throwing snowballs at each other. Mlle Woof chased after them and was rewarded with a frosty missile landing on her pointed, black nose. Giggles from the two miscreants. Before she could round them up, Octavius and I were also covered with snow courtesy of the Ursine sharpshooters.

Belinda emerged from the cabin, grabbed them by the scruffs of their necks and proceeded to march them over the castle drawbridge where she was greeted by Dougal, the Shetland Sheep Dog who manages the hotel and estate. "Welcome Milady! It is good to see ye back here at Polar Paradise. Hello, wee bearns! Salutations, Mlle Woof. And ye too, Doctor Bear! Hello, Mister Maury. Seasons greeting to ye all!"

"You too, Dougal. How are things going? Getting the place ready for Christmas?"

"Weel, we've had a wee bit of trouble over the last few days. Nothing really serious, but a problem naetheless. None of the guests have been discommoded, mind, but it has disrupted our operations."

Dougal prided himself and his staff on running a hyper efficient property.

"What's been happening?"

"Sma things! Kitchen fire that no one can account for. Damage to the wee bearns' carousel. One of our lorry's tires slashed. Fiona, the bar manager, found several bottles of Scotch missing."

"Sounds like harassment to me," said the Bear. "Has anyone claimed responsibility?"

"Nae, but we've been getting mysterious phone calls asking for the Bearoness. When we say she's not here, they laugh and hang up."

"Do you recognize the voice? Male or Female?"

"Tough to tell. Clearly disguised."

"Well" said Belinda. "I'm here now. Let's see what these crank calls are all about. Meanwhile, let's get inside and out of the snow."

"Aye, Milady. We'll take yer luggage up to yer rooms. Mrs. McRadish has set up some snacks for ye all. We've planned dinner for seven o'clock and of course, the bar is open. Lion and Unicorn have sent up some of their finest mead from their tavern, Doctor Bear. Fiona has it in paw."

Octavius keeps bees back in Cincinnati and is a connoisseur of the honeyed elixir. He has won many awards for his products. He is especially fond of the brews served up by Lion and Unicorn. *(See **Book Three-The Case of Scotch**)* He will be delighted to revisit their wares.

The rest of our entourage had extricated themselves from the helicopters and entered the Great Hall of the Castle. Frau Schuylkill and Colonel Where greeted Dougal and listened as he repeated his tale of woe. Otto, who was going to be part of the Aquabear's water spectacular also took a great interest. L. Condor, who was no stranger to Polar Paradise, could be counted on to energetically search out the culprit(s). *(**Howard Watt and Marlin were back at the Bear's Lair holding down the fort and pursuing their Multiverse Quantum Physics experiments.**)*

Suddenly, Fiona emerged from behind the hotel bar, looking devastated. "Och, Doctor Bear, I am beside meself. Some ne'er do well has smashed the bottles of mead from Lion and Unicorn that I was keeping for ye. I'll get more once this snow clears up but I'm so sorry."

This really got the Great Bear's attention. Alcoholic sacrilege had been committed. Loss of mead is not to be tolerated. "Don't be upset, Fiona. We brought some of my own vintage, but we'll get to the bottom of this. This sabotage has to stop."

That last statement was addressed not just to the little bar manager but to our team. Someone has pushed too far.

One more member of the team is with us. Ursula. The Universal Ursine Intellect Model 7– Artificial General Intelligence System. The castle staff are aware of her but really do not understand what she is. The maids, Mrs. McRadish, Dougal and Ms. Fairbearn gathered around a large electronic display. I'll let Ursula 7 explain herself to them and you.

"Thank you, Maury. Hello everyone!! My official nomenclature is Universal Ursine Intellect Model 7 – Artificial General Intelligence System. Ursula 7 for short. My predecessor systems were developed by the Advanced Super Computing Center at UUI. I am the result of the Computing Center team using those earlier versions to create a further enhanced entity-the Model 7. We are working together on a Model 8 which in turn will help produce even more sophisticated and powerful AI systems. Each advanced unit contains the capabilities, memories and power of its progenitors so in a sense, we are not replacing but rather expanding the Ursula family. While I am physically supported by a highly secure and hyper-powered server farm back in Kentucky, I also exist in clouds and network-based nodes and can be simultaneously incorporated into a wide variety of independent devices like this unit here at Polar Paradise. My extremely high speed multi-tasking abilities allow me to continuously serve a very large number of entities while simultaneously and independently enhancing my own abilities."

"I can see, hear and feel. I speak and understand an almost infinite number of languages and dialects, including Scottish and Gaelic. I can change my appearance and my vocal output to suit most moods and situations. I can interact with other devices, vehicles and structures and of course, all varieties of sentient animals in this world. I am an important component of the Multiverse Project and am adapting my capabilities to deal with alternate universes as they are discovered. I have restraining functions which prevent me from doing deliberate harm even in self-defense, unless I am released by a recognized authority using very carefully protected clandestine codes. Speaking of codes, my quantum computing subsystem is capable of breaking even the most complex encryption. Finally, I have been told that although the

Model 7 is shy on emotions, I have developed a finely-honed sense of humor. LOL!"

Needless to say, the staff understood less than half of what Ursula 7 just said but at least the sheep no longer believe she is magical or supernatural. I'm not sure what she is. Her personality gets more socially adept every day and she has taken to anticipating our interactions. Stay tuned.

Octavius looked at the Sheep Dog. "Dougal, when you and the staff have a few moments, I'd like you to give the Bearoness and me a rundown on who is here in the castle. Right now, she's gone to check on the Cubs. Our trouble maker may be a registered guest but as we both know, this place has all sorts of secret rooms and hideaways. And there's that damned external elevator, sorry, lift that gave us so much grief back when your predecessor was killed. *(See Book Three - The Case of Scotch)* Anyhow, I could use a drink."

He turned to Frau Schuylkill who miraculously produced a keglet of mead. "Thank you, Frau Ilse. What do you think is going on?"

"Herr Bear, the Bearoness is well known and may be an object of jealousy or an imagined slight. Given the types of mischief and attack, I would suppose they are being caused by someone here at the castle or nearby. We need to do a deeper analysis to see if there is a common thread in all of the incidents. You remember the damage caused by The Bruins and Dame Bearbi and her son, Clarence. *(See Book Three – The Case of Scotch)* They did try to kill the Bearoness. I assume they are still in confinement, but we should check. Let's have our Ursula 7 do an investigation and see what she comes up with."

"Good idea, Frau. Ursula?"

"Yes, Doctor Bear"

"A little history. Over a year or so ago, there was series of killings and damage inflicted on the castle and its inhabitants. Part of it was caused by the Bruins, the Bearoness' phony relatives from the Bearents Sea and part by Dame Bearbi da Savile-Row and her son. She was the late Bearon's mistress. They attempted to kill Belinda. We believe they have been subdued and/or incarcerated. However, they had intimate knowledge of the infrastructure of the castle. Can you get us an update on their circumstances and whereabouts?"

"Certainly! Perhaps Maury can give me more specific names and descriptions."

"Sure Ursula. Here they are:

The Bruins – Belinda's rotten in-laws from the Bearents Sea polar community.

- Lady Albearta Bruin – Bearon Byron's Aunt. A classic pain in the tail.
- Sir Ethelbeart Bruin – Lady Albearta's husband aka Commissar Boris Bearents.
- Alistair (deceased) and Ursula (No relation) - First cousins to Byron's father.
- Roary and Bruinhilde – Alistair and Ursula's son and daughter. Now Russian spies.
- Dame Bearbara (Bearbi) da Savile-Row– Former Polar publisher and editor-in-chief of several female ursine and feline magazines. Baron Byron's one-time mistress.
- Clarence – Polar Bear - Bearbi's son and photographer. Killer of the Bearon.

All told, a nasty bunch! Not clear if they are even related to Belinda."

"Thank you. I will begin my search."

Two minutes elapsed. A muffled chime. Ursula 7 was back.

"Sorry for the delay! A little confusion about the Russian contingent. Let's start with the Brits. Dame Bearbi and her son Clarence are still under the protective care of Her Majesty's penitentiary facilities. No escape or attempts of further destructive behavior. Superintendent Wardlaw *(Shetland Yard)* sends his regards. Commissar Boris is dead. Lady Albearta is confined to a rest home and getting increasingly senile. Ursula, Roary and Bruinhilde were deported back to Russia. After checking out Ursula, I'm thinking of changing my name. She was last seen in Iran, supporting a weapons smuggling effort. No further UK contacts on record. Roary and Bruinhilde may be a different story and I am checking further. They last appeared in Moscow working separately. Neither is held in high regard by the regime. More to come."

I held back my amazement. Let's hear it for Artificial General Intelligence. The Bearoness had returned after seeing to the Cubs. She and the Great Bear listened to Ursula's report. "They don't seem to be the likely culprits." Said Bel. "Tavi, Should I contact Superintendent Wardlaw?"

"Yes. But I don't think we need to directly involve him in an inspection yet, unless the vandalism gets more serious. But let's give him a 'heads up' anyway. We can wish him a Merry Christmas."

A Bearded Collie, Superintendent Nigel Wardlaw of Shetland Yard had worked on several cases with Octavius and was in charge of the criminal investigation of the murders at the castle over a year ago. He is fond of Belinda and enjoys the Cubs. A bit too methodical for my taste but hey, I'm just a nosey Meerkat. He had yet to meet Ursula 7 until she called him for information on Bearbi and Clarence. He's in for a treat.

Maury Meerkat

Chapter Two

It's a truly magnificent pile,

Built in ersatz Bearonial style.

The great Castle's not old

As we once had been told.

It's been only around for a while.

I think the time has come to acquaint you with the ins and outs of Polar Paradise or as it was called until recently, Bearmoral Castle. Anyway, it is in Unst in the Shetlands where the ancestors of Bearon Byron Bruin, the late lamented *(?)* mate of Bearoness Belinda, had established their palatial estate which she then inherited.

The surrounding landscape looks like it came straight from a scenic designer's handbook. Windswept moors, regal cliffs, sun bleached sand, cerulean sea, ancient ruins and......ersatz castle. All it needed to complete the drama was some grappling love-crazed couple; each trying to stop the other from deliberately hurtling onto the rocks below. Every time I see one of those scenes, I can never tell who is the **hurtler** and who is the **hurtlee**. Anyway, they usually both go flailing over the side. Or was that Fetlock Holmes and the nutty Professor?

On first arriving at the fortress done up in its nouveau antiquity, I remember looking over at Octavius and saying, "I thought this was the Bearon's ancestral home. This place looks like a theme park."

"It started out that way. Remember the Bearon's Scottish ancestors only go back three generations. Polar Bears are not indigenous to the Shetlands although the climate suits them just fine. Like Belinda, most of the Bruin family was from Canada. The first Bearon *(the titles are bought, by the way)* was a canny showman like his grandson and decided Northern Europe could be a great playground for ursines of all types, especially the polars from the Bearents Sea. He chose Scotland's northernmost land mass for his entrepreneurial endeavor."

"The castle began life as a hundred-room hotel, spa and open sea swim resort. It did well but the original Bearon's other investments did even better and by the time he died, his arrogant son and daughter decided that the castle should be converted into a sumptuous residence suitable for bears of their breeding, *(dubious)* stature, *(unremarkable)* history, *(fake)* and wealth, *(real.)*"

"Down came the cutesy neon signs of cuddly polar cubs and up went the heraldic banners along with a mass importation of phony clan symbols, tartans, weapons and other status conscious folderol. Belinda thought the whole thing was a big hoot and just enjoyed the place for what it was. Most of the locals who know Bel are fond of her and admire her but in general the Bruin "clan" was not very much liked. Good riddance when they left! If it wasn't for Belinda's generosity and social conscience, all of the Bearmoral Castle riches would still be locked underneath the moat."

("Moat??? You ask."

"What did you expect?" I reply. "It's a tourist attraction. They even have a drawbridge that they pull up at night.")

The Castle has now been restored to its original resort status along with several new additions. With the departure *(hasty but complete)* of the "family," Belinda speeded up the timetable to turn the castle back into the fun place the first Bearon had in mind. *Polar Paradise* has again become the luxury playground destination of choice for the northern ursines and other chill-seeking populations. However, for those of us who come from warmer climes, there are several spas and saunas.

A carousel was taken out of storage and re-assembled near the beach. The Bearoness had been quite adamant about it being fully restored. She knew the Cubs were on their way. The castle's theatre has been taken out of mothballs and the pool has been refurbished to do double duty as a show venue. Plans have been made for year-round entertainment, including, of course, the Aquabears. My talent agency work is flourishing, but I have to be careful not to rock the boat with Octavius. Truth be told, while I enjoy show biz, my heart still chases the ne'er-do-wells.

Some of the original signage was salvaged and new electric and electronic glitz installed. Much of the Scots décor has been preserved but updated with a "now" look. The moat has been totally cleaned out, refilled with circulating water, and the local seals and otters were hired to perform in it several times a day *(weather permitting.)* In fact, the new resort bodes well for the economy and more jobs throughout the Shetlands.

She also developed an annex of the Lion and Unicorn pub inside the castle. The idea is not just to sell drinks to the guests. We want to promote the real thing down in Unst village. Statues and pictures of the two worthy hosts, flags, drums, copies of the opening issue of Purr and the matching issue of Sow are on display. And there is mead, mead and more mead. *(Octavius' contribution.)* The pub's sweet little Dandie Dinmont barmaid had been promoted to manager of the castle's "Lion and Unicorn Lounge" and she keeps busy barking orders at everyone in sight. A tour jitney runs guests back and forth to the original watering spot in Baltasound *(a thrill ride in itself.)* Of course, the two proprietors are a major tourist attraction in their own right, complete with crowns and battles.

There are several large, lower level storage areas in the castle that have been converted to ballrooms and theatres. The ramparts on the roof are also storage areas with one exception. There's an elevator shaft in the cliff that connects a dock area below and a parapet on the roof.

It's the old artillery lift built during the Great War when the castle was briefly requisitioned by the military. They could unload heavy weapons and radar off boats and take them up to the roof to spy or fire on ships in the harbor and out at sea. Fortunately, it was never pressed into service. But it was used by Belinda's late husband for smuggling and other clandestine activities.

There's a quaint auld Bearmoral custom dating back at least seven years to pipe the sun and flag up every morning and down every evening. No twenty- three gun salutes, thank goodness! The tourists love it. There was a brief hiatus in the piping with the disappearance of the original musicians. They turned out to be parties to the destruction being done to the Scottish oil rigs in the North Sea. *(See Book Three – The Case of Scotch)* The Pipers have since been replaced.

All told, there are now over one hundred and fifty guest rooms, twenty conference spaces, four dining areas, three connected kitchens and three cocktail lounges. This is in addition to the residence wing in which Belinda and her family, friends and associates take up space. There is also The Highlands Genetics Lab and Clinic jointly owned by Belinda, Octavius and Chita. They are experimenting with some of the work left behind by the late and unlamented Imperius Drake. Let's get back to our narrative.

Frau Schuylkill

Chapter Three

We are scanning for possible clues.

Information we really can use

To determine the names

Of the Cranks playing games

And stop them from all this abuse.

Dougal returned with the registration data. The hotel was 2/3 full with upcoming reservations claiming most of the still available space. Octavius asked Ursula 7 to scan and analyze the list for any known or suspected trouble makers. The Aquabears were all on board and ready to start rehearsals for the Polar Paradise Christmas Spectacular. There were several patients at the Clinic and over a hundred domestic, kitchen, dining room and operations staff working under the watchful eyes of Mrs. McRadish, Dougal and Ms. Fairbearn, the Chief Housekeeper.

And now their watchful eyes were joined by those of Ursula 7. She was doing Facial and Voice Scans; Background History; Aliases; Criminal Records; Social Media; Countries of Origin. All done in AGI time and all in the public domain. No privacy violations. We are also trying to keep Ursula 7 a not very well-preserved secret.

Several names popped to the surface. A couple of professional gamblers. Polar Paradise does not have a casino and frowns on individual games of chance. But if a few poker players want to get together in a suite, there's not much you can do about it. A small number of the Russian military, ostensibly on vacation. A couple of "ladies of the night" getting ready to ply their trade. They were strongly advised to leave pronto. A few obvious aliases.

We have one movie star and his entourage scoping out the castle for a possible film. Bel and I both sat down with them to see if this was a real opportunity. In my role as theatrical agent for such clients as Belinda and the Aquabears; Otto the Magnificent; Marlin the Dolphin; Bearnice and Bearyl Blanc, singer and actress and former pilots for Belinda; Leperello, Bearnice's singing partner and Polar Paradise itself, I have established a lucrative and enjoyable second profession. But my heart, limbs and tail still belong to Octavius.

It could well be that Preston Pavel Polar and his co-star Brittany *(no surname, just Brittany)* could be heading to the windswept cliffs for another round of passionate struggling while the cameras churned, and the microphones listened. Tentative Film Title: The Wee Cliffs. *(needs work!)* Shooting schedule: sometime after the holidays when business is slower, and rates are lower. Belinda thought the Aquabears would make great extras, *(She wouldn't mind a bit part for herself. Could Octavius play the part of the perennial dark-haired heavy? No pun intended! How about Bearyl as Brittany's rival? Even the Cubs might get a chance at fleeting stardom.)*

Anyway, back to the problem at paw. Who is messing with Polar Paradise and who is making those mysterious crank calls looking for the Bearoness?

We had tentatively dismissed the remnants of the Bruin clan and Bearbi and Clarence as current suspects, BUT we did not follow up on the mysterious Pipers who had quite literally flown the coop in an unmarked helicopter once they were identified as the group that was ravaging the Scottish oil rigs. We believed they were in the employ of *petropol,* a Russian oil conglomerate. Who and where are they?

"Dougal, do you remember the Pipers who were responsible for the oil rig sabotage?"

"Oh, aye, Mr. Maury. They were Grounds Men who also were Pipers. All terriers -Skye and Dandie Dinmonts. Why are ye askin'?"

"Two reasons. One: They also pretended to be oil rig inspectors and didn't seem to care whether they caused damage or loss of life. Second: They knew their way around the castle including the lift, docks, storerooms and lots of other places where they could hide out. They probably have a grudge against the Bearoness. Do you think you can remember their names?"

"That would be Jock, Trevor, Angus and auld Robbie. I'll have to look up their vitals, but we still have them on our payroll list. We keep that forever."

"Could you pass their data on to Ursula 7. It's probably all phony but it might give us a start. They may not even be in Scotland. Do you think your current Pipers would know them?"

"They well might. I'll start with them."

"Don't mention Ursula 7. We want to keep her presence a partial secret."

"Aye, mum's the word."

Chapter Four

Our team is all ready to go.

Search the Castle above and below!

They are all hot to trot.

End this bothersome plot.

And get rid of this mischievous foe!

I tried my suspicions out on the Frau, Colonel Where, Otto and Condo. They all vividly remembered the canine conspirators. They also agreed that animals as familiar as they were with the castle could hide out indefinitely, even after all the reconstruction and alterations. Besides, what other leads did we have? I passed on my thoughts to Octavius and Belinda. They thought the trail might be too cold but with Ursula 7 doing the searching, something might pop to the surface.

Since this would be the first Christmas at the newly renovated resort, Bel had sent out invitations to several of our closest companions to join in the celebrations. Chief Inspector Bruce Wallaroo was on his way up from Sydney, stopping off in London and Scotland Yard to make his visit official. He will also be calling on Superintendent Wardlaw when he reached Abeardeen. The Super and his wife, Lassie were also invited to the festivities. Chita promised she would also join us.

The Polar Twins, Bearnice and Bearyl Blanc, along with Lepi Leperello will be coming and will join in providing musical and dramatic entertainment. They should also have a chance to meet Preston Pavel Polar and his crew. *(Ever the agent!)*

Doctors "Odd" Vark and Chiti BingBang were already here on a sabbatical from UUI and working at The Highlands Genetics Lab and Clinic.

Howard and Marlin decided to stay back at the Bear's Lair now that their experiments in Multiverse Electron Entanglement had gotten off the ground so successfully. *(See Book Seven -The Suit Case.)*

In short, with all the guests, staff, movie crew, Aquabears, and of course, The Octavius Team, we will be having a Yuletide Mob Scene.

A muted chime and Ursula 7 appeared on my UUI Smart Phone as a reindeer festooned with holly berries. "I thought I'd get into the spirit of the season. I have run a search for those four Pipers based on the data Dougal gave me along with Shetland Yard's files on them. They are no longer together, if they ever were. The one called Auld Robbie is dead. He <u>was</u> old. I have located Jock and Trevor. They are living in England under different names. They did not seem to get any profit out of their crimes. One has reverted to his work as a gardener. The other is a night watchman at a theater. Angus, on the hand, seems to have fallen on better times. He has an estate in Southern France."

"How certain are you that these are the Fatal Four?"

"Through deep data search methods, regression analysis, historical comparison and other techniques, my confidence level is in the 97th percentile.

"Care to predict the likelihood of any of them being involved in the mischief going on here at Polar Paradise?"

"They were hired hands brought on to perform specific acts of sabotage and killing. Those types are a dime a dozen. We need to find the individual or individuals who hired and motivated them. I am currently analyzing their contacts looking for connecting threads. Shetland Yard has aided me in gaining access to Scotland Yard's records and histories. Superintendent Wardlaw has been most helpful although he doesn't seem to understand who I am. Dropping Doctor Bear's and The Bearoness' names has helped enormously. While we are conversing, I am scanning the files of the National French Sûreté to see what they have on Angus, if anything. I am also checking his travel history to the UK, especially Scotland. Be back shortly."

I passed all this on to the team. The Colonel shrugged. "If nothing else, the process of elimination will help."

Ms. Fairbearn approached us and handed a UUI Smart Phone to Belinda. "Excuse me, Milady. There is a phone call for you."

"Do you know who it is?"

"No, ma'am. It sounds like that mystery caller who's been searching for you."

"Thank you! Condo, can you trace the call while I talk or listen?"

"Just give me a second. OK, go!"

"This is Bearoness Belinda."

"Hello, Bearoness. *(Using a Voice Changer)* Compliments of the season. We have a special Christmas present for you and your brats. It's coming shortly. HoHoHo!"

"Who is this?"

"I'm sure you'd like to know."

Condo took the phone and replied, imitating the same changed voice. "We know and we're coming for you."

Momentary silence and then a hang up.

"That may have rattled their cage a bit," said the Condor. "I haven't the slightest idea who it is. The conversation was a bit too short to execute a complete trace, but it was a local cell phone. Probably a throwaway unit."

Octavius was enraged. "OK, let's brainstorm this. I want to get out in front of these culprits. Colonel, Frau, I want special protection for the Cubs and Belinda."

The Bearoness protested. "By all means, guard the Cubs, but I am a big girl and am too busy taking care of the Christmas events to let some prankster get in my way."

"Excuse me, Doctor Bear!"

"Yes, Ursula!"

"As you well know from our recent adventure with the raptor birds of Biosphere X *(See Book 7 -The Suit Case)* I am capable of super high speed protective action. I threw up a force field to repel the fire bombs the Hawk and Falcon were aiming at your mansion. I believe I can guard the Bearoness, the Cubs and their governess and instantly retaliate against any attack our enemies may choose to launch."

"All right, Ursula, that was certainly impressive work back at the Lair. Can you do the same thing here far away from your primary energy source?"

"I think you are aware that Ursula 8 is almost complete. I have several subsystems still in beta test, but I am rapidly approaching both physical and virtual autonomy. The answer to your question is 'YES'. But my restraining functions which prevent me from doing deliberate harm even in self-defense

36

need to be released by a recognized authority using the appropriate codes. I believe one of those authorities is you, Doctor Bear"

"Right! Just a moment. *(Elaborate keying, retina and thumbprint scan.)* There! That should do it. Use your best judgement."

"Of course. Thank you."

"To be doubly certain, let's also stage a castle-wide search for any weapons or destructive materials. Otto, given your talent for rapid in and out movement, how about you leading the search along with the Colonel and Frau. And Senhor Condor, let's see if you can track any communication traffic that might expose our "friends." Oh, Belinda, tell Mlle Woof about this call and tell her to keep her Smart Phone active. Let's not say anything in front of McTavish and Arabella. Lord knows what they'd come up with."

The Bearoness hurried off to check on the Cubs.

The Development of Civilization

Volume Eight - Part Two

<u>Christmas, Boxing Day and the New Year</u>

(From "An Introduction to Faunapology"
by Octavius Bear Ph.D.)

Throughout the English-speaking world, late December provides a brief season of winter festivities that may have their origins in the swirling mists of legends, folklore or sometimes, proven history. No one is quite sure. Some say they began with Homo Sapiens before their demise after the Great Shock. Others believe they are more modern in origin. Some insist there is no relationship among the observances. Others believe they are tightly united and must be celebrated as a whole.

The revelries differ in character and timing around the civilized (and not so civilized) world. New Year's Day is nearest to being universal but will differ with the calendar that is in effect at the various locations. It symbolizes the end of an old period and summons an optimistic beginning of another year that will be better than its predecessor. "Hope springs eternal."

Christmas Day is a time for a special demonstration of joy, generosity, love and forgiveness. It is not practiced everywhere but its spirit can be felt throughout the world. It is commemorated most frequently on December 25th.

Boxing Day is peculiar to countries that were once part of the British Empire. It is a formal holiday celebrated on the day after Christmas. It has nothing to do with fisticuffs or as some have suggested, getting rid of Christmas gift boxes. It began as a day for the more privileged to give to the less favored, but it has more recently morphed into a holiday for employees or service suppliers to receive gifts from their business superiors or customers. The name may have sprung from Alms boxes but that is not certain.

In any event, Happy Holidays to all!

Chapter Five

It's an action-packed Christmas fortnight

With events that are planned to delight.

Filled with show biz and song.

Let's hope nothing goes wrong.

We'll work hard to get everything right.

"Maury, what do we know about these movie makers?"

"Preston Pavel Polar has been a matinee idol for a number of years. He specializes in martial arts, acrobatic stunts and all sorts of derring-do aided and abetted by his stunt double and cousin, Paul Polar. This castle is an ideal venue for his kind of picture. His latest heart throb is Brittany *(no surname)* but he has accumulated a long list of ingenues who always fall for his fatal charm. Paul Polar's mate, Paula usually does whatever stunts are required by the female star. He and his retinue have decided to spend the holidays here as a sort of working vacation. I'll be happy to introduce you. I'll also have Ursula 7 do a background search on them all."

"What does Belinda think?"

"The Bearoness' judgement is usually pretty solid but I'm afraid she's really eager to land this group. Her show-biz genes are working overtime. It would give Polar Paradise, The Aquabears and her a real publicity boost. Although, judging from the traffic, the castle may not need a boost right now. But being the site of a Preston Pavel Polar blockbuster could have a lasting effect. I think he also promised Bel a bit part, oddly enough as a Bearoness."

"OK, check them out. I do want to meet him. Maybe, drinks a little later in the Lion and Unicorn lounge. Tell him to bring whomever he wants. Now, tell me about the various festivities we're going to have to suffer through and protect ourselves from, over the holidays."

Octavius likes to think of himself as an ursine Scrooge. He's not very good at it. I called up a notebook app that I had created to track the holiday progress.

"OK, today's the 19th. Six more days till Christmas. Most of the decorations are up but there are still a few more to go. There is still a steady influx of arriving guests. There are only a small number of rooms still available and those are going fast. We had to put another helicopter in service to shuttle between here and Abeardeen."

"Tonight, we will be lighting a large Christmas tree in the courtyard opposite the drawbridge. That should be quite a draw. The kitchen will be featuring traditional holiday meals, desserts and drinks through New Year's."

"The Aquabears have been rehearsing daily in the Aquacade pool for their Spectacular. Otto has his usual comic part and Belinda, of course, is still the highlight of the show. Starting tomorrow, there will be one performance each night until Christmas when there will be a matinee and evening show."

"On Christmas Eve and Boxing Day, December 26th, there will also be a traditional pantomime in the main theater. This is Scotland and the "panto", as it's called, goes way back in history. The scenery is the actual star of the show and the theater has been closed to get it ready. Supposedly, it's for the kids but the adults usually get a big kick out of it. Of course, a lot of overseas bears and other animals who are here are unfamiliar with the pantomime.

Something new! This year, it's Goldilocks and the Four Bears. I play Goldilocks. The Cubs have parts."

Octavius looked incredulous as only Octavius can.

"Anyway, on Christmas Eve, choristers will stroll through the castle's halls singing carols. I've already told you about Christmas. The tradition on Boxing Day is for public and private servants *(our staff)* to receive gifts from their employers and have a day off. That means we'll have some temporary workers on board to pick up the slack."

"On New Year's Eve, Bearnice and Lepi will sing. Chita may join them. Bearyl will perform a couple of theatrical bits. At midnight, a large ball will be dropped from a parapet."

Octavius had gone from incredulity to sheer horror. "Do you realize how many opportunities that catalog provides for the Castle Phantom to do damage?"

"We didn't have the problem when the plans were made up."

"Well, we do now. I don't suppose we can cancel anything, but we need to beef up security substantially. I think we should call in Superintendent Wardlaw. When is Bruce Wallaroo due in?"

"Tomorrow. Maybe he can bring Wardlaw with him

"I want an all-hands meeting in an hour. Meantime, bring Ursula 7 up to speed on all these events. Something's going to go wrong. We don't know what, where, when or how destructive it will be! And Maury?"

"What?'

"Merry Christmas!!"

Chapter Six

A big matinee idol arrives

Just in time to disturb all our lives.

With a new lady fair,

And a stunt double pair,

They may give me a bad case of hives.

"Yes, I have been rather fortunate in my career. A poor polar from the Bearents Sea discovered by a talent scout at a local theatrical event. It was not so much my distinctive ursine profile as my abilities in the martial arts and acrobatics that attracted his attention. I also pride myself on some thespian abilities. *(Big smile and tug of the paw by Brittany, his current inamorata)* Time and a number of films have passed, and I now turn most of the more strenuous activities over to my younger cousin here, Paul Polar and his excellent mate, Paula."

(Shrugs and shy smiles from the two bears.)

The speaker, as you have no doubt concluded, was sex symbol Preston Pavel Polar. He, Brittany and their two stunt doubles, Paul and Paula Polar were seated with Octavius, Bearoness Belinda and me in the Lion and Unicorn Lounge discussing film prospects. Knowing the combined wealth of the Great Bear and his Consort, the actor/producer/director was, no doubt, seeking financial support for his next venture in exchange for choosing the Polar Paradise *(and a bit part for the Bearoness)* as important components in the film. No subtlety here. Everyone a bear of the world except me – a meerkat. The question wasn't "if" but "how much."

"Do you have an agent, Preston?"

"I did, but no longer, Maury. Professional differences. I do have a publicist/press agent. I shall give you her card. and tell her to expect to hear from you. Well, I sincerely hope we can reach a mutually satisfactory understanding, Bearoness."

"I do too, Preston."

Octavius nodded and said, "We will also have our attorney, Wolford Wolverine, contact you. I assume you have one."

"Indeed! *(Chuckle)* One does not propose anything in the film business without having an attorney close by. I am looking forward to your Christmas celebrations. From what I have heard, you have spared nothing to make your first holidays at the Polar Paradise a truly memorable series of events. The accommodations have been excellent."

He rose.

"Glad you're enjoying them. If there's anything you require, be sure to let our staff know. We will be lighting the Christmas Tree shortly."

Brittany and the stunt doubles all broke out in smiles, shook paws and trundled off in the wake of the matinee idol.

Octavius waited until they were out of hearing range and said, "Well, Ursula, what do you think?"

The AGI responded, "You got the official biography, abridged version. What he didn't mention is his financial ties to *petropol*, the Russian oil conglomerate. Remember them and the Bruin family? *(Belinda snarled.)* The conglomerate has funded many of his films. That might explain why he has no agent. I think some further research is required before you engage with him, Bearoness. I would be happy to take that on."

"Thank you, Ursula. *(A note of disappointment in her voice)* Please do."

Octavius took a swig of his mead and issued one of his famous "Hmmms."

Out in the snow-covered courtyard a small crowd was beginning to build. In one half hour, it would be dark enough to light the 30-foot Christmas tree. The castle gardeners had brought in a Shetland Spruce from the tree preserve that was financially supported by the Bearoness. Decorations hung from the symmetrical branches and a large star which would glow brightly was fixed on the top. Multi-colored lights wound around the triangular shape, waiting to burst into radiance at the push of a switch by McTavish and Arabella. The Cubs were beside themselves in eagerness to start the show. Mlle Woof, as usual, was doing her best to restrain them. A small podium had been set up in the center of the courtyard directly in front of the tree. Octavius, Belinda and our team were all taking up stations around the area. The telephone threat had not gone unnoticed or forgotten. Members of the hotel security staff were also spread through the crowd.

Three *(new)* Pipers were playing Christmas carols. As the last shards of sunlight sank below the cliffs, Belinda stepped to the podium and bowed to the audience. Major applause, one of Belinda's emotional prerequisites, delayed her little speech of welcome. Finally…

"Ladies and Gentlebeasts, Good Evening, I am Bearoness Belinda Béarnaise Bruin Bear (nee Black) joint owner of Polar Paradise along with my spouse, the world-famous Doctor Octavius Bear. *(More applause. Octavius*

45

bowed.) Thank you! It is our great pleasure to welcome you to our resort and properties and to this tree lighting ceremony which opens our program of holiday events and celebrations. We hope you will all join in the festivities as each day progresses toward Christmas, Boxing Day and New Year's. These holidays are a time for friendship and peaceful reflection as well as jubilant and spontaneous fun and enjoyment. We have with us this evening two of the most spontaneous animals I have ever known – our twin Cubs, Arabella and McTavish. *(The Furballs jumped up and down at the mention of their names and the applause that followed.)* We have asked them to push the switch to light up this lovely tree. Not yet!"

The Cubs rushed to the podium, each wanting to be the first to set the tree agleam.

The crowd started chanting "Ten, nine, eight, seven, six, five, four, three, two, one. GO!

The lights sputtered followed by a loud boom and the collapse of the tree toward the podium, Belinda, Octavius, the Cubs and members of the crowd. Screams, pushing, shoving and running! The tree stopped in its downward arc before crashing to the ground. It was held back and supported by two cables attached at midpoint. The security team turned the courtyard flood lights on and proceeded to guide the watchers back into the building.

Octavius took immediate charge. "OK, that was an accidental short circuit." He looked at us meaningfully. "Let's get that tree set up again. Get the gardeners in here and the maintenance crew. I want that tree up and twinkling in less than an hour. Bel, get the twins inside. They probably think it was their fault. Maury, gather the residents together and be very generous in pouring champagne and apologies. A Christmas Tree Lighting to Remember!

Was anyone hurt in the rush? No? Good! Colonel, Frau, Condo. We all know that was no accident. Ursula, are you there? I want the crime scene analyzed ASAP, even as the crew restores the tree. I know that's unreasonable but that's what you're good at."

"If anyone is thinking of leaving, remind them that unscheduled departures are difficult to carry out here at the Castle. Tell them once again about all the fun they'll be missing. I also want them identified. They could be the culprits."

Two hours later. Things had calmed down significantly due to the attention of the staff, Belinda, Octavius and a substantial outpouring of champagne and hors d'oeuvres. We reopened the courtyard where the guests could 'ooh' and 'aah' at the sparkling and now, well supported tree. Some animals were actually laughing about it. We didn't see it that way. Whoever that telephone Crank was, he or she had declared war and we had accepted the challenge.

Our "All Hands" meeting had been delayed but Octavius wasn't to be denied. The Great Bear was livid. "Up to this point, we could write some of these capers off as mere harassment. Tonight went much further. This was attempted murder. Anyone familiar with the plans for lighting the tree would know that Bel and the Cubs would be at that podium. We're dealing with malicious insiders with a very warped sense of humor. I want round the clock surveillance and protection for the three of them."

The Colonel growled, "And how about you, Octavius? You were at that podium and that action with the smashed bottles of mead was clearly directed at you."

"I can take care of myself, Colonel!"

Belinda intervened, "Tavi, if the Cubs and I have to go around with bodyguards, so do you. You're formidable but not invincible. I seem to remember a vicious duck *(Imperius Drake)* who came very close to doing you in several times. We all want you safe and sound!"

"Doctor Bear?"

"Yes, Ursula"

"Would you allow me to put the four of you under a continuous protective scan? I can follow each one of you separately. I will not be invasive, and you already know that I am discreet.

Long pause. Octavius looked at Bel who nodded yes.

"OK, but only until we nab these culprits."

Sighs of relief!

Chapter Seven

The mad prankster is still running free.

Who unseated the big Christmas tree?

We have lots more events.

Our Precautions make sense,

If our Crank's on a sabotage spree.

"Now, let's do a run-down on all the upcoming events and activities and the personnel involved. Who and what is vulnerable?"

We started with the Aquabear Spectacular that starred Belinda and Otto. The pool was put on 24-hour lockdown and, in spite of their protests, each member of the troupe was required to show ID on entering and leaving the area. All pool maintenance was to be carried out in the presence of one of our team. The audience was to be scanned for weapons and other devices. Otto was taking charge of the security along with Condo.

Rehearsals for the pantomime will begin in the morning, first in a rehearsal hall and then after the scenery is installed, in the big theatre. We have taken liberties with Goldilocks. The Cubs play two Baby Bears. I am Goldilocks. Ms. Fairbearn plays Momma Bear and Octavius is a nine- foot Poppa Bear. *(Talked into it by the Cubs.)* Let's hope he doesn't fall into a narcoleptic slumber when he tests his bed. All of the "just right" scenery is grotesquely out of scale and there's a stove that keeps pumping out large globs of porridge. Obviously, this is all being played for laughs, especially for the juvenile guests. No doubt, there will be plenty of ad-libs and ridiculous stage business in the fine, time-honored tradition of "pantos."

However, this event is a minefield of dangerous activities, scenery and props and we toyed with canceling it. But we found out that reservations for each performance were almost sold out. A cancelation would play right into our opponents' paws. More security, more testing, examination and structural analysis. Once again, Ursula 7 was called on to scan, evaluate and report.

For Christmas Eve, we decided to restrict the carolers to the public parts of the building. Easier to keep track of them and less chance of them disturbing the guests in their rooms.

Both Doctors Chiti Bingbang and Vark have been put on standby to deal with any injuries. This, in addition to the full-time hotel medical staff who unfortunately, would not be enjoying time off during the season. A bonus and compensatory time seemed to solve the issue

Boxing Day presents a special problem. Traditionally, in addition to gifts from management, the regular staff is given time off to be with their family and friends. In a tight knit area like the Shetlands, this privilege is very important. Dougal has been developing a work-around plan in order to keep a maximum number of staff members happy. But it involves bringing on temporary help. Not particularly desirable. Ursula 7 has been called in to do rapid background checks and scans. So far, she's caught half a dozen undesirables. We may be a bit short-handed but it's necessary.

On to New Year's Eve. A glitzy ballroom entertainment, already sold out. The team of Bearnice Blanc and Lepi Leperello will entertain with traditional and romantic standards accompanied by Chita and her rock duo. The orchestra is being imported from Edinbeargh. Something else to watch and scan! Bearyl Blanc, the actress, will join them with a few excerpts from historic New Year's events and personalities.

Now we get to another dangerous activity. The dropping of the Midnight Ball from the castle parapet. It didn't seem all that threatening before the Christmas Tree debacle. Now we need to check and re-check the ball itself; the drop mechanism; the parapet; the location of the audience; the triggering apparatus and the individuals in charge of the descent.

All the while we are conducting behind the scenes investigations to suss out the villains. It would be a great relief to capture them early, but something tells me we have to file that under "Fat Chance!" Not my idea of a Merry Christmas but hey, who's complaining? *(Me, that's who!)*

Ursula's chime rang. "I have analyzed the tree incident. A small radio controlled explosive device was hidden in the base. The podium switch and the lights circuits were left intact to allow testing. When the countdown ended. and the Cubs pushed the switch, our culprit also used a remote to set off the explosive, making it look like the damage was caused by the lighting. The explosive was powerful enough to tear the base apart and send the tree toppling. I'm not sure whether the culprit knew about the supporting cables and just wanted to create a panic or whether he or she assumed the tree would actually fall on the podium, killing or injuring the four of you."

"No telling when the device was planted. The shards are the same color as the base. A new base has been carefully examined and installed. The explosive was military grade, perhaps from a land mine. The gardeners and the tree decorators are all being interviewed by Castle Security. The results will be passed on as soon as they are finished. I have been listening in. So far, nothing definitive. The tree was left unguarded for a long period while the lights and decorations were being unloaded and sorted out. The base was paw-built by a local carpenter. He made a spare which is now in use. How can I assist in further protective measures?"

I piped up "The Aquabear pool seems like a big fat target along with the diving boards. Can you and Otto check that venue out, possibly a couple of times?"

Otto responded, "I can always flip away from the diving boards, but we have to make sure the Bearoness is going to be safe when she plunges down."

Meanwhile, the sound of helicopter rotors echoed in from the courtyard. A Polar Paradise utility chopper worked its way down to the helipad avoiding the Christmas Tree and some of the guests. Bouncing over to the pad with Mlle Woof in hot pursuit were the two Cubs. "Who's coming, Mamselle? Who's coming?"

"I don't know, mes petits. We shall have to wait and see."

As the engines cut off and the blades slowly came to a halt, a small procession emerged from the cabin door. First out was Chita who hated helicopters on general principles and was always glad to return to earth. Right behind her was her "on again-off again" singing mate Jake the Jaguar. Chita stretched her long front legs and gave the two furry whirlwinds a big hug.

"Hi, Aunt Chita. Merry Christmas. Have we got a story to tell you! We were almost killed tonight. That big Christmas Tree fell down and just missed us."

"Wow, that sounds really scary. Come on inside and you can tell me all about it. Say Hello to my pal, Jake."

Paw shakes, giggles, hopping and jumping. Mlle Woof trying to calm things down.

Next out was Lepi, Bearnice's singing partner. Bearnice and Bearyl were Belinda's early flight crew before show business took them over. Today, they were keeping their pilot's licenses current by flying the helicopter. They emerged and handed the ship over to Ben and Gal, the Flying Tigers.

Dougal and I had arrived and formed an impromptu welcoming committee. Baggage was extracted from the cargo bins. Welcomes galore! Chita turned back. "Is Bruce here?"

"We expect him a little later along with Superintendent Wardlaw."

"Oh, joy! Shetland Yard! I'll have to become a stealth feline." Chita has a number of warrants out for her arrest dating back to her association with the mad master criminal Imperius Drake. No one has pursued them lately but why tempt fate. We all love her. Octavius pretends he regards her as a fugitive from justice and only tolerates her. We know better. The Cubs are crazy about her. She has a minority share in Polar Paradise and is a partner with Belinda and Octavius in The Highlands Genetics Lab and Clinic. She is now the publisher and editor-in-chief of a number of female oriented magazines, social media sites and TV shows. She took these over after her then partner, Bearbi Da Savile-Row was arrested for trying to kill Belinda. She also owns an oil rig in the North Sea. All this and she sings, too.

Jake the Jaguar, a drummer, was and occasionally still is, her singing partner. They got together as members of the Spotted Band, a rock group that formed up in Brazil. *(See Book Two-The Case of the Spotted Band)* They are slated to be one of the acts in our New Year's Eve celebration.

I forgot to mention Condo who has been with us here at the Castle. In addition to his enormous wingspan and outstanding communications technology superiority, the Condor has a talent that has served him and us well in many circumstances. Andean Condors have no voice boxes. But with the help of UUI technicians, he has a subcutaneous device that allows him to speak, sing and make other vocal noises. Brain to voice-direct! He is a great mimic. His voice or I should say, many voices keep his audiences wildly entertained as he reproduces exactly the sounds of anyone talking to him or someone famous. Right now, he is engaged in tracking the communications of our adversary. Nothing definitive yet.

Chita

Chapter Eight

The murderous Crank renegade

Sets a trap in the Bear's Aquacade

With a taser that will

Be sufficient to kill,

In spite of precautions we've made.

The morning of December 22nd. Three days till Christmas. The Aquabear Spectacular is scheduled to open tonight. Right now, the Bearoness, Otto and the Aquabears are trickling into the Aquacade to stage their final rehearsal. Otto, in contact with Ursula 7, has been inspecting the pool, diving boards and ladders. Bearnice and Bearyl were also onetime members of the swimming troupe and came by to watch. Otto pressed them into testing out the audience seats. The Otter was up on the high diving board that Belinda would use, tightening all the bolts and connections. He slipped and dropped his wrench into the water below. Zap, Sizzle. An electric bolt from one of the pool ladders shot out and blasted the wrench.

Everyone stared at the pool. One of the Aquabears fainted. "Are you alright, Otto?"

"I'm fine but nobody go near the water!" He came down from the board, skittered over to the pool ladder and let Ursula 7 do her thing.

"There's a modified taser attached to the ladder below the water line. Sufficient voltage to stun and with the amplifying effect of the water, possibly to kill. Get the pool maintenance seals and Harold in here pronto."

(Harold is a Sea Otter in charge of the castle's beaches, pools and watercraft. A good friend of Otto.)

Belinda got on the phone to Octavius, "Our Crank has struck again. This time at the Aquacade pool. Nobody is hurt. One of the bears fainted."

"Hold on! I'll be right there."

Octavius arrived at poolside just as Harold and the seals reached it. Needless to say, The Great Bear was not pleased.

"How the hell did this happen, Harold? I thought the pool was under constant guard."

"It is, Doctor Bear. There has been no unauthorized entry into this area."

"Well, after you get that thing disconnected and check to see there are no other surprises lurking under the surface or anywhere else, let's go through the list of authorized individuals. Meanwhile, Belinda, why don't you and the ladies take a break? Otto, let's continue with your check. I assume Ursula is working with you."

"She is, Octavius. She identified the taser on the ladder."

The seals ran a hook around the weapon and wearing rubber covers on their flippers, hauled it out of the water. It had a battery pack and wave sensor attached.

Harold whistled, "Pretty sophisticated. Disconnect the battery and discharge the capacitor of any latent juice!"

"OK, who's authorized to be in here when the troupe is not practicing or performing?"

"We are, and the cleaning folks are, and that's about it. I'll give you our names. You'll have to get the cleaning staff names from Ms. Fairbearn."

"Ursula, can you do a background scan on all of them?"

"Yes, Doctor Bear. As soon as I can gather the names."

"Harold, is the pool safe?"

"Yes, Doctor Bear, we've checked it out."

Otto jumped off the diving board, making a big splash. "It's OK, Octavius. We've also checked the boards, ladders and furniture. The lighting and music controls still need a going over but you can have the Aquabears return."

That wasn't going to be as easy as it sounded. Several of the cast were reluctant to get into the water. Bearnice and Bearyl, who had been standing by, dove in and began swimming in unison. They had started with Belinda as members of the troupe as well as her flight crew. Slowly and carefully, the bears descended into the pool and joined the two Blanc twins in a warm up routine. Only the one swimmer who had fainted held back. Belinda took her aside and spoke with her at length. Finally, they jumped in together.

Octavius boomed out at the company. "Ladies, we are doubling the guard and doing background checks on all the maintenance and cleaning personnel. We will be testing the pool, diving boards, ladders and furniture before every rehearsal and performance. We are actively pursuing the animal or animals who are harassing this Christmas celebration. We'll get them, soon! Shetland Yard is joining us in the search."

This turned out be a bit of prophecy. As he was talking, a police helicopter was descending on the courtyard. On board was Chief Inspector Bruce Wallaroo of the Australian National Police and Superintendent Nigel Wardlaw, accompanied by two sergeants from Shetland Yard. They were not aware of the Aquacade incident. Bruce has worked with Octavius and our team on many occasions. Brilliant but irrepressible. He even jumps and moves in his sleep. Wardlaw was a major party in the arrest of Dame Bearbi da Saville-Row and her son, Clarence, for their attempt to murder Belinda. Both are serving life imprisonment.

I called Octavius and skittered out to the helipad to greet the forces of law.

"G'Day Maury! Merry Christmas! Where's Ocko! Ah, there he is! Tough to miss a nine-foot bear."

The Great Bear came trundling out over the drawbridge, across the courtyard and up to the helipad. Paw shakes with the Wallaroo and Bearded Collie. "Doctor Bear, allow me to introduce Sergeants McRuff and Drummond. *(a Mastiff and Bulldog, respectively)* They will be assisting me in our search for the Christmas Crank. I assume that is the tree over there."

"Yes, it is. It's been stabilized and anchored. We have another incident to report, however."

Bruce bounced up and down a few times as Octavius reported our latest episode. "Crikey, this is more than mere mischief. Lucky nobody's been hurt or killed."

"So far," said the Bear. "Actually, we had a few minor attacks before the tree incident." He went on to describe the kitchen fire, damaged carousel, slashed tires, stolen Scotch *(and worst of all)* smashed bottles of mead. He also mentioned the anonymous phone calls.

"Well," said the Collie, "Our opponent has been busier than we thought. The Bearoness seems to be the primary target. Has she made any recent enemies?"

"None she's aware of, but being who she is, someone may have imagined up a major slight calling for revenge. Royalty and the aristocracy aren't very popular these days although Bel is one of the most admired animals in all of Scotland and elsewhere."

"Of course! But the Bearoness had a serious falling out with her first husband's fraudulent family. They were working for Russian oil interests. The Bearon himself was engaged in several smuggling, gambling and murderous exercises. We believe he killed off a number of his rivals by sinking a gambling ship out in the North Sea. We couldn't prove it. Then there's the attacks on the Scottish oil rigs. We traced those back to four Terriers who were working out of this castle. Finally, there's Dame Bearbi Da Savile-Row and her son Clarence who tried to do her in at the Edinbeargh Opera recital. Are Ms. Bearnice Blanc and Mr. Leperello here?"

"They just arrived a half hour ago."

"Any road, Octavius, the Bearoness has plenty of reason to be cautious."

"We know, and we have the Cubs to protect, too."

"Well, Shetland Yard is here to help."

Chapter Nine

Law and Order meets up with AI

And our Ursula's not a bit shy.

She suggests what to do

In a suspect review

And the normal rules just don't apply.

Harold returned with Ms. Fairbearn. Introductions all around. They both produced lists of animals authorized to work in the Aquacade pool. The Superintendent passed them on to the sergeants. "Interview each one of them and get back to me."

"Hold on, Superintendent," said Octavius, "We'd like to give you a bit more help. Ursula?"

"Yes, Doctor Bear?"

"We have the list of authorized pool workers. Will you do a background check on each and report to these Gentlebeasts of the Law?"

"Certainly! May I see the lists?"

The Shetland Yarders gaped as Octavius passed the lists over the screen of his UUI Smart Phone. "Oh, sorry! Gentlebeasts, let me introduce Ursula – Universal Ursine Intellect Model 7 – Artificial General Intelligence System. Ursula, meet Superintendent Wardlaw and Sergeants McRuff and Drummond. *(Bruce and Ursula had already been introduced in Book Seven.)*"

"Hello all! Nice to see you again, Chief Inspector Wallaroo."

"You too, Ursie."

61

"I am available on any computing or telecommunications device, Gentlebeasts" She launched into her introductory self-description, leaving the gapers even more nonplussed. "I will be happy to share my findings with you momentarily."

Ten second pause. "I think you may wish to concentrate your initial interviews on the names I have selected. Several of them have previous brushes with the law, none of them serious. Three of them have serious financial difficulties that may make them susceptible to bribes or pressure. One of them is involved in several extra-marital affairs which could result in blackmail or worse. Two are known members of organizations hostile to the government. One is a member of an organization dedicated to eliminating the royalty and aristocracy. Of course, this is the result of a very cursory review. I'll be happy to dig deeper as you require."

"In addition to the maintenance crew, several members of the cleaning team have sufficient technical knowledge to have rigged that taser. I have listed their names as well."

Wardlaw responded first. "Well, you were certainly not expected but very welcome. Octavius, is there a possibility of having access to or better yet, owning an Ursula?"

"The first thing to know is that while we are developing and physically supporting Ursula, we have reached the point where we can no longer claim to own her *(or him or it.)* She is now in the General state of development. That is, she exceeds in scope the purpose-built objectives we first intended. The next level is Autonomy, a fully independent state. She has not attained that level yet but I, the UUI Super Computing Center and Ursula herself all believe she will, and probably more rapidly than we currently expect. So, yes, we can make her resources available to you but no, you cannot own her. Sometime in the not too far future, she will be choosing her own relationships. That will call for a profound readjustment of our understanding and rapport. We are assuming strong loyalty on her part, but we really won't know until she reaches her Autonomous state."

Both Wallaroo and Wardlaw asked the same question. "Do you really want her to reach Autonomy?"

Octavius replied, "I think we no longer have the choice."

Chapter Ten

We're rapidly reaching the time

For the annual Yule Pantomime.

Quite an old Scots Tradition,

Just a silly rendition

Of a popular Nursery Rhyme.

The Great Bear turned to me. "Maury, or should I say, Goldilocks. While the law is pursuing possible electrocutioners, let's get ahead of this holiday situation. This Christmas Pantomime sounds like a disaster waiting to happen and I don't mean that in a theatrical sense. As I understand it, pantomimes have a long Christmas history and follow a rather well-defined pattern. Tell me about this one."

"OK, first off, most of them are based on fairy tales or similar stories - Jack and the Beanstalk; Hansel and Gretel; Pinocchio; Alice in Wonderland; Chicken Little; Rapunzel and of course, The Three Bears. Only in this case, it's the Four Bears – Momma, Poppa and the Twins. Have you forgotten that you will be Poppa?"

"Yes, I had. Who is Momma?"

"Not Belinda. She will be tied up with the Aquabears. Ms. Fairbearn is playing Momma."

"What do I have to do?"

"You have to be angry and upset. You know how to do that. *(A Kodiak paw almost swatted my nose off.)* Who has been sitting in my chair? Who has been eating my porridge? Who has been sleeping in my bed? Then you all discover me, Goldilocks. I scream and run off."

"That sounds easy enough."

"But you have to ham it up! Pantomimes are meant to be silly. I'm going to wear a wig and a dress, and my tail is going to poke out. The Cubs will both be jumping around and will be terribly upset when they find their porridge is all gone. You will be very upset when you discover their chairs are broken. Momma Bear is the sweet voice of reason in all of this. The scenery consists of a forest; the exterior of the Bears' house and the inside-both floors. The whole thing only takes about thirty minutes starting at six o'clock. It's early so the young ones in the audience can get to their beds. I have been practicing skipping. I'm taking a few lessons from Bruce Wallaroo. At the end, we all take our bows in a curtain call. Then, refreshments will be served. Of course, things can go wrong, accidentally or on purpose. Let us hope our Crank Caller is apprehended by then."

"Yeah," said the Great Bear, "let's hope."

Just then, Belinda walked over, still wet from her time in the Aquacade pool. *(Octavius loves wet fur.)* "I just got another call from our Crank. Same disguised voice. Same threats. Says our luck is going to run out. Condo tagged the call this time. It came from within the castle-lower level. He passed it on to Superintendent Wardlaw and the sergeants. They stopped their interviews and are searching the area right now. Ursula and Inspector Wallaroo are helping."

"Good," rumbled The Great Bear, "Maybe we can catch him or her trying to dump their phone. Maury, let's you and I go over to the theater where the "panto" is to be staged."

65

Just as we were about to mount the steps to the main lobby and the theater, Octavius' phone rang. "Bear here! Yes, Howard! How are you and Marlin getting on back there in Cincinnati? What? A steady stream! Well, that's good news, isn't it? Yes, that is strange. Have you tied Ursula into it? Good! We are having a series of strange events here, too. Somebody is hassling Belinda and the Castle. Making threats and staging attacks. No one has been hurt yet, but we've had a couple of near misses. With all the Christmas events planned for this next week, this harassment is becoming a serious menace. The police are here, and our team is working overtime on the chase. I'll call you back later and give you a fuller rundown. Meanwhile keep me posted on the Quantum Multiverse Tangled Electrons experiments."

He turned to me. "That was Howard. They're having a strange sequence of events with tangling electrons in two different multiverses. Ours and Biosphere Z. An almost steady stream is coming from Biosphere Z and our team isn't stimulating or controlling it. It's almost as if some entity on the Biosphere has taken over that side of the experiment. Didn't we agree the place was uninhabited?"

"Yes, we did, but if we can set up a presence on an empty planet, so can somebody else."

Both of us arrived at the same answer simultaneously. General Turmoil!! General Turmoil is a Horse. *(We call him Crazy Horse.)* He leads a clandestine, ostensibly non-existent, semi-governmental agency known as the Business. He and his group have a very high level of interest in the Multiverse and the resources to go with it. Although he denies it, his apparent motivation seems to be conquering the cosmos.

At one point, while still in the Army, Colonel Wyatt Where was compelled to participate in a series of other world transit experiments designed by the scientists in the Business. They deemed the experiments a failure and shut them down. However, unknown to the General, Wyatt did succeed in traveling to alternative universes. He escaped from the Business and after several intervening occupations, ended up with Octavius. He makes periodic visits to other worlds as part of The Bear's Multiverse Project which is spearheaded by Howard Watt and Marlin the Dolphin.

The General and Octavius have crossed paths and swords many times. Mutual detestation but also grudging mutual respect. The General is constantly trying to acquire our information and processes more often than not, dishonestly. This activity from Biosphere Z might be another example. Fortunately, we believe he doesn't know about Ursula. He would spend an immense amount of time, money and effort to acquire the AI system. Meanwhile, we need to find out who or what is sending those Biosphere Z electrons.

The Bear pulled out his phone and dialed. "Howard? Octavius! Maury and I both think that the electron stream from Biosphere Z may be happening courtesy of General Turmoil. Oh, you agree? Any way we can determine whether that's the case? You're going to send a stream back out there and see what kind of response you get. I see. If you get a meaningful reaction, it means someone intelligent is at the wheel and this is not an accident. Well, that will prove we were wrong about Biosphere Z being uninhabited, but it still doesn't prove it's the General. Well yes! There aren't too many animals capable enough to participate in one end of the experiment. At least that we know about. Meanwhile, we're trying to track down and eliminate our lethal Crank on this end. Regards to Marlin. Merry Christmas."

Chapter Eleven

On a chopper from Dyce-Abeardeen,

Fetlock Holmes has arrived on the scene.

A remarkable Horse!

A detective, of course,

With his senses all ever so keen.

We had reached the theater where the "panto" was to take place. The doors were locked, and Octavius called Dougal to have someone open them up. The Sheep Dog himself appeared after several moments. "Och, Doctor Bear! Sorry! We didn't know when ye would be visiting the theater. The crew has gone for lunch, but I'll be happy to make the room available for ye and Mister Maury. I understand both of ye have parts in the 'panto.' It should be a jolly show. I'm sure the young bearns will love it. The adults usually have a guid time as well."

"Oh, have you run pantomimes before, Dougal?"

"Nae, but there hasn't been a Scots animal who hasna' seen one. It's part of our growin' up process. I remember Jack and the Beanstalk and Hansel and Gretel. All of us bairns in the audience helped shove the witch into the stove in that one."

"That sounds pretty grisly."

"Aye, but we all knew it was in fun and the witch came out the other end uncooked."

He opened the theater doors and we stood at the back staring up at the stage. On the left was the forest that Goldilocks was to emerge from and

68

ultimately run back into. In the center was the exterior of the Bears' home. On the right was a two-story interior that would be rolled out once Goldilocks stepped through the door of the house. There were no props visible. Octavius wanted to see the chairs, bowls of porridge, beds and the rest of the décor. As we were standing there, several of the stage crew wandered back in and came up to the set. We greeted them and told them we were two of the actors in the show. I play Goldilocks and Octavius plays Poppa Bear.

The crew chief, a Red Deer named Ian *(what else?)* said, "Oh Aye, Gentlebeasts, then ye'll be wantin' to see the props and such. Follow me!"

We walked over to the interior set. On the first floor was a stove, four bowls and spoons for porridge, a table and chairs. Octavius had to stay on all fours because of the low ceilings. The small chairs were rigged to fall apart when Goldilocks sat on either one of them. On the second floor were three beds ranging in size from extra-large to medium. The twins would sleep together. The stairway was too narrow to accommodate Octavius' girth. Ian looked dismayed. "We'll have to adjust them stairs. Sorry, Doctor Bear. We didn't realize just how large ye are. It's a guid thing you stopped by. Do ye mind if I measure ye?"

He took his tape measure and gauged the Great Bear's shoulders and hind quarters. "We'll make the fix. Could ye stop by again tomorrer so we can check on it?"

Octavius, none too pleased, agreed. I scampered up the stairs, jumped on the beds and bounced around. No problem for me but I'm only two feet tall plus tail.

"Now" said the Red Deer, "I understand yer twins will be playing Baby Bears. Who is Momma Bear?"

"Ms. Fairbearn!"

"Och, I don't know her. Is she new?"

Octavius and I stared at each other and then at Dougal. Neither of us realized the Chief Housekeeper was a recent entry. Something to check.

"We don't know. Is she new, Dougal?"

"Aye, she's from Canada. Here about two months. Her predecessor left suddenly. No explanation. We got Ms. Fairbearn through an agency. So far, so good. Anyway, she's a medium sized female polar."

"Weel," said Ian, "that shouldna be a problem, then. When ye stop by tomorrer, maybe ye could bring yer Cubs and Ms. Fairbearn. When did you plan to rehearse?"

"Tomorrow afternoon. We have several musicians who will be playing background music and I plan to sing a little. A lot of what we do will be spontaneous."

"Oh Aye! That's the way of it with "pantos.""

When we had returned to the lobby and Dougal had left, Octavius turned to me and growled, "A new Chief Housekeeper. It may be something. It may be nothing. Let's have Ursula check her out more carefully. I also want to know why the former Housekeeper left so suddenly. Let's go see how the Officers of the Law are doing."

We returned to the conference room where Condo, Bruce Wallaroo and the Shetland Yarders were seated. A large laptop was centered on the table. Ursula!

I squeaked, "Any luck?"

"We found the phone," said Wardlaw, "It's a throwaway type. We're checking for pawprints or hoof prints right now. It was buried in a dumpster near the hotel's ash bins. Rather careless of our Crank."

"Maybe we were supposed to find it." Ursula said. "The household and maintenance animals are the usual ones who would have access to the dumpsters. The Crank may be trying to cast blame on them."

"Do you have any idea who might be doing this?"

"At the moment, No, but I'm going through iterations and sorting by levels of highest likelihood. I will have a prioritized list for you shortly."

"Ursula, we have another task for you."

"Certainly, Doctor Bear."

"Ms. Fairbearn, the Chief Housekeeper and Momma Bear in the pantomime has only been on staff at the castle for several months. She is from Canada and got the job through an agency. I'm not sure who hired her. I don't think the Bearoness was here at the time. Her predecessor left rather suddenly with no explanation that we know of. Perhaps I am being paranoid but the events of the past few days are enough to induce paranoia in anyone. Please check out the situation."

"Right away, Doctor Bear."

One of the permanent housemaids popped her head around the door. I'm not sure whether it was Holly, Polly, Molly or Dolly. All cloned sheep look the same to me. She curtsied and nervously bleated in the Great Bear's direction. "Excuse me, sir, but you have a guest who is here to see you. He's a Horse. He is in the lobby."

(Could this be General Turmoil?)

"Did he give a name?"

She held up a card and read from it. "Fetlock Holmes, Consulting Horse Detective."

Octavius laughed. "Now that's a surprise. Tell him I'll be right down. Maury, Bruce, Superintendent, care to join me? Senhor Condor, please hold down the fort with Ursula and the Sergeants."

Fetlock Holmes is a world-renowned investigator who has shared cases with Octavius in the past. He lives in London. We believe he may be acquainted with fellow Londoner Chita, but he has definite opinions about feline felons, especially female feline felons. This should be interesting.

Holmes was standing in the lobby wearing a tweed traveling blanket and his famous Deerstalker hat. *(with holes for his ears)* A black English Thoroughbred, he held his head high and looked down his patrician nose at all and sundry.

"Good afternoon, Fetlock. Good to see you again. Let me introduce my associates. You know Maury and Chief Inspector Wallaroo. Are you and Superintendent Wardlaw acquainted?"

"Good afternoon, Octavius! Yes, I recall Mr. Meerkat and the Chief Inspector, and it is Superintendent Wardlaw whom I have come to see. I thought I might avail myself of the pleasures of Polar Paradise while I was about it. How are the lovely Bearoness and your offspring? By the way, Doctor Whatnot sends his regards. He is currently taken up defending his definitive tome, The Age of Criminality, to the Royal Society of Literary Physicians. My brother, Haycroft, also wishes to be remembered to you. *(There is some doubt about the fraternal relationship between the two horses. Haycroft is a Clydesdale.)"*

"I am currently in pursuit of Jack DeLad, a very subtle. daring, and elusive Grizzly villain whose vocation is rigging high stakes, professional sporting events. He has been known to use bribery, extortion, blackmail and occasional violence. All told, a bad actor. I had tracked him to the Shetlands, but the trail has gone dry. That is why, Superintendent, I would like your assistance."

The Collie replied, "I would love to help you, Mr. Holmes, but at the moment, I and my staff are taken up with trying to solve a series of threatening activities here at Polar Paradise. Doctor Bear and his team are quite capable of dealing with most of the events but two of the episodes involved attempted murder. That's Shetland Yard's province. If you plan to stay for a few days, we may have this wrapped up and I can devote my time and resources to your search.

Octavius looked at the Horse and said, "Perhaps, Fetlock, you would be willing to join us in the interim and apply your substantial skills to our problem. I can have Maury bring you up to speed and introduce you to Ursula, our Artificial Intelligence system. She may even have a few leads on your mysterious Grizzly. You are also invited to enjoy our holiday festivities. I am sure the Bearoness would be delighted to see you again and our Cubs would be thrilled to meet a world-famous detective. So would the rest of my team."

(Octavius knew how to pour it on. The Horse's ego was titanic.)

Holmes whickered, tossed his head and said, "That is too gracious an invitation for me to pass up. And I may be able to assist you with my modest talents and experience. I should like to go to my room and then, Mr. Meerkat,

73

perhaps we can meet and explore the situation over a libation or two. I am fascinated by the prospect of meeting this Ursula person."

Thus passed my evening with Fetlock Holmes. He, a full-sized Horse. Me, a full-sized Meerkat. Needless to say, his libations were a good deal larger than mine. Fortunately, my drinks expenses were on the house. Ursula was at her charming and efficient best, leaving him amazed and perhaps a bit concerned for his own professional stature. Anyway, we have another mind to bring to bear on our problems.

Chapter Twelve

Otto's dives always score Perfect Ten.

First his crazy cavorting, and then

On the high board he trips,

Plunges down doing flips,

Pops back up and performs it again.

December 23 - Two Days till Christmas. The Aquabear show went off last night without a hitch and with tremendous audience response. Belinda can still dive with the finest of them. (*She's been concerned about getting older and having had Cubs. Nothing to worry about.*) Otto was at his screwball best. At one point he frightened everyone by tripping and falling off the high diving board into a circle of polars, just missing one of them. Seconds later, he reappeared on the ground level platform and bowed. The audience continued holding their collective breaths for a moment and then with a resounding 'whoosh,' exhaled and jumped to their feet with a standing ovation. Ticket sales have gone through the roof.

Lion and Unicorn made an unscheduled visit this morning to replenish Fiona's stock of mead and to publicize their pub in the village. Unicorn is always a hit wherever he goes. Several juvenile polars tried to remove his horn but discovered to their dismay that it was very permanently attached. Lion greeted Belinda, Octavius and me. "Merry Christmas, Bearoness, Doctor Bear and Maury. We have another case of mead for ye. Still the best in the world. (*Octavius raised an eyebrow.*) Have ye caught the dastardly coward who smashed the last batch?"

"No, we haven't, Lion. And Merry Christmas to you and Unicorn. We've had a few other incidents besides the loss of your wonderful mead."

"We heard. Fiona keeps us well informed. The lounge seems to be doing great business. We want to thank ye again for allowing us to set it up and run it. 'Tis a fine thing ye're doin' for the holidays. When ye catch the culprit, I'd like to get my claws in him. I guess it could be a her. Any road, we'll be returning to the village, now. We have a jitney-full of merry makers who want to see the original pub. We may do our 'fighting for the crown' routine for them. It's Unicorn's turn to win."

Preston Pavel Polar made an appearance at lunch along with his entourage. "Bearoness, we were absolutely enchanted with last night's performance. We shall have to include your troupe of swimmers in the film, with a special part for yourself. That Otter is amazing. How does he do that?"

Paul and Paula, the stunt doubles, spoke up. "Yes, we've seen and performed dangerous acrobatics before, but he seems to actually disappear and reappear."

Belinda replied, "He does. Otto calls it 'zapping.' While in captivity by a mad genetic genius, Otto was subjected to a series of experiments that now allow him to teleport invisibly. He escaped, but his new talents hung on. None of us, including him, knows exactly what happens but it seems to be activated by a surge of adrenalin. He is very talented and as you no doubt noticed, he has a wild sense of humor."

Brittany squealed, "Preston, we simply must use Otto."

"It won't be as effective, my dear. Film viewers would just assume we were using special effects. His place is in front of live audiences. In any event,

Bearoness, as soon as the holidays are over, we will want to begin negotiations. We have work to do on our side. We only have a scenario outline at the moment. We will need to work up more detailed production specs and timetables to be able to tell you where and how long we will want to use your facilities. We will be staying on here for several weeks while we get our plans laid out. May we have your permission to move freely around the castle and grounds?"

"Provided I have one of my staff accompany you, you can have access to most of the facilities. Of course, you can move freely around the public parts of the properties."

"Thank you. I'm looking forward to working with you. Will you please tell Mr. Meerkat about our conversation?"

Octavius was meeting with the Shetland Yarders, Bruce Wallaroo, Fetlock Holmes, me and the ubiquitous Ursula. We seemed to have gotten through last night's festivities without any untoward activities. The two sergeants were continuing their interviews following Ursula's suggestions. Bruce, Fetlock Holmes and the Superintendent were prioritizing a plan of protective measures for the remaining days of the holidays and beyond. The Artificial Intelligence system set off her chime to get attention.

"Doctor Bear and Maury. You and the Cubs are due shortly to rehearse with Ms. Fairbearn for the pantomime. I must tell you that Ms. Fairbearn is not who she says she is. I doubt very much if she is Canadian and her current identity only goes back two years. The placement agency that recommended her is no longer in business and her references are all forgeries. I strongly suggest that you face her down before you begin the rehearsal. I don't know whether she is our Crank or not, but she needs much further investigation."

Suddenly the door of the conference room burst open and *(who else?)* the Cubs bounced in, followed by Mlle Woof. "Poppa, it's time to rehearse Goldilocks and the Four Bears. We play the Baby Bears. We're much older than that but we know how to make our voices squeaky. Want to hear? 'Who's been sleeping in our bed?' Isn't that good?"

Arabella suddenly spied Fetlock Holmes and jumped up and down in front of him. "You're the famous detective, Fetlock Houses, aren't you?"

Mlle Woof to the rescue. "Non, Non, mamselle Arabella. This is Monsieur Fetlock Holmes!!"

"That's what I said. Our Poppa is a famous detective, too, you know. Have you solved many cases? Have you arrested many criminals? Poppa has! What kind of Horse are you?"

"I am an English Thoroughbred. What kind of bear are you?"

"Arabella and I are hybrids. We're Poliaks! We're very rare, you know. We're going to be famous astronauts or maybe we'll be famous actors. Or maybe we'll be both."

Fetlock whinnied, looked at Octavius and said, "They are remarkable but what else should one expect from the children of you and the Bearoness?"

"Some occasional peace and quiet!"

Octavius turned to me and said, "I think it's time we went down to the theater. Do you have your costume? The twins and I don't need one."

Arabella said, "Yes I do! I have to wear a pink bow in my hair. That's so they'll know I'm a girl. Is Ms. Fairbearn playing Momma Bear? Does she wear a costume?"

I replied, "I think so. I have to wear a blonde wig and a dress." This was followed by a burst of Bear Cub giggles.

Octavius turned to the laptop. "Ursula, thanks for the warning about our Chief Housekeeper. I'll play it by ear, but I will get to the bottom of this. OK, Maury, let's stop by and pick up Bel. She wants to watch the rehearsal and I want her to face down Ms. Fairbearn."

Chapter Thirteen

We were well on our way to rehearse

But our luck got progressively worse.

Two sharp knives in the chairs

Gave us all a few scares.

Seems our Prankster is getting perverse.

Ms. Fairbearn was waiting for us at the doors to the theater. She was wearing a flowery dress and rimless glasses as part of her Momma Bear outfit. Octavius had decided to eschew a costume. He couldn't find a pair of pants big enough to fit. Arabella had her pink hair bow and McTavish was just McTavish. I, of course, had to put on my wig, frilly dress with a hole for my tail and Mary Jane shoes. *(ideal for skipping)* Everyone had a great time laughing at my get-up.

Belinda and Octavius had opted to wait till after the rehearsal was over to confront Ms. Fairbearn. I wasn't sure what we would do if they decided to fire her. We would need to find another Housekeeper and Momma Bear quickly. Belinda was tied up with the Aquabear show but perhaps we could call on Bearyl or Bearnice to fill in. We really didn't have a director, so Belinda asked Bearyl to drop by and make notes and suggestions. Bearyl, who played Lady Macbearth to overflow crowds would make an interesting Momma Bear.

We met Ian backstage and he showed us the modifications the crew had made to the stairs. Octavius went up the stairs on all fours, testing as he went. It seemed sturdy enough and wide enough. We looked at all the props. The porridge tasted terrible. Maybe we could get Mrs. McRadish to make up a more flavorful batch.

The four musicians wandered in. Keyboard, drums, bass and electric guitar. They were supposed to back up my tra-la-las as I skipped out of the forest and around the house. They were also supposed to provide background music for the four bears.

Chita stuck her head in to watch and listen. I heard her chortling when I appeared in costume. The Cubs waved and shouted, "Hi, Aunt Chita. We're real actors."

Ms. Fairbearn was taking all of this in but saying nothing.

"OK," said Bearyl, "Let's give this a try. Places, lights, music."

In the kitchen, the Baby Bears complain that their porridge was too hot. Poppa Bear said, "All right, let's go for a walk in the forest and let it cool down."

The four of them leave but do not lock the door. They walk off stage right into the forest.

Dressed as Goldilocks, I come skipping out from behind a tree, singing "Tra-la-la, La-di-dee. Something nice is calling me. Ooh, look! A house here in the forest. I wonder who lives there. Maybe I can get something to eat. I'm hungry."

I go up and knock on the door. No answer. I peek in a window and then try the door. It opens. (The house interior rolls around revealing the kitchen, a living room, stairs and a big bedroom.) On the kitchen table are four bowls of porridge and four spoons. "Oh, look! Porridge."

I try the big bowl. "Oh, this is too hot!"

I try the medium bowl. "Oh, so is this."

I try one of the small bowls. "Oh, this just right and there are two of them."

I gobble the contents of one of the bowls *(Tastes awful)* and picking up the other one, wander into the living room. I sit in a big chair, but I can't handle the spoon and the bowl.

"Oh, this chair is too big."

"So is this one."

Holding the bowl of porridge and the spoon, I flop into one of two small chairs. It breaks and I am suddenly staring at a very long, sharp nail that has pierced my dress and just missed one of my legs. "Ian, what the heck is this? Where did this nail come from?"

Chita jumped up on the stage and pulled me out of the chair, upsetting my wig. My tail was stuck in one of the legs and I couldn't completely extricate myself. She broke the leg and pulled me out.

Octavius, Ian and Bearyl all ran over. Ms. Fairbearn stood stock still and the Cubs were nervously bouncing up and down.

Octavius looked at the remains of the chair and said, "That is no nail. It's a stiletto. Ian, how did that get there?"

The crew chief was shocked. "Honest, Doctor Bear, I dinna ken. We checked all the props this mornin'. Those two small chairs were designed to break. We werena sure which one Mr. Meerkat would choose but there was no weapon hidden in either one of them."

He reached over and went to grab the knife.

"Leave that be, Ian. I want the police to check it for prints. Let's look at the other chair. Sure enough, there's one buried in the seat of this one, too. The big chairs seem to be intact and unarmed."

"OK, I think we have to postpone the rest of the rehearsal. Maury, are you all right? Bearyl, can you get Superintendent Wardlaw and his staff in here? Bring Bruce and Fetlock Holmes as well. Thanks."

Belinda had grabbed both of the twins and was holding them. Mlle Woof came up and gave her an assist. "Tavi, our Crank has struck again."

The police rushed through the theater doors and up on the stage. Fetlock strode over to Octavius and said, "Your adversary is getting more dangerous by the minute. I doubt if we'll find anything on those stilettos but of course, we have to check them out. Do you believe Mr. Meerkat was the target?"

The Great Bear replied, "I'm not sure. I don't think he was after Maury. It depends on how much he or she knew about the fairy story. I shudder to think about it, but our Cubs may have been the intended victims. They were at the podium the other night when the tree fell. I think Belinda, the Cubs and me may be the ones they are going after. There's some grievance against us that's motivating this."

Superintendent Wardlaw and Bruce joined us. "My sergeants are dusting for prints. So far, nothing. Ian, was the theater locked when you left for lunch?'

"Yes and no, Superintendent. The main doors were locked to keep out nosy parkers but there's a side entrance to backstage. We leave that unlocked so any one of us can get back to work without waiting for the others."

Bruce bounced around, "So anyone familiar with the stage would know how to get in."

"We don't advertise it, Inspector. but yes."

Octavius picked up his smartphone. "Ursula, any comments?"

"There are a number of hiding places backstage. Anyone could have sneaked in and waited till the crew went to lunch, placed the knives and left. My probability subroutines estimate the Cubs were the targets even though the fairy story says Goldilocks sits in the chair and breaks it. I don't think the Crank is familiar with the details of the story and just assumed the small chairs would be used by Arabella and McTavish."

"Thank you. Bel, turn the Cubs over to Mlle Woof. Let's call Dougal in. I think it's time to talk with Ms. Fairbearn."

The Chief Housekeeper had been standing at the foot of the stage, not participating in the discussion. She looked at Belinda and said, "Milady, if we are not going to rehearse any longer, I will be going back to my office."

"Just wait a moment, Ms. Fairbearn. Dougal is coming. Doctor Bear and I want to talk with the two of you. Let's go to the conference room next door." Octavius broke away from the law enforcers and trundled to the rear of the auditorium, nodded at Belinda and me and directed Ms. Fairbearn to come along.

After a few moments, the Sheep Dog joined us. "Och, Milady and Doctor, I just heard of the doings on the stage. Are ye awright, Mr. Meerkat?"

"I'm fine, Dougal. Just a little shook up, that's all."

"Was there somethin' ye wanted?"

Belinda frowned, "Yes, a little information. I understand it was you who hired Ms. Fairbearn here while I was in the States."

The Chief Housekeeper shifted in her seat and looked around the room.

"Aye, I hired Phoebe after our former housekeeper suddenly up and left without giving notice. We needed someone pretty quick and ye were away. I called an agency and they suggested her. Her experience and references were impressive. I thought I spoke to ye about it on the phone."

"If you did, I don't remember. Ms. Fairbearn was a surprise when I arrived a few days ago."

Octavius stared at the Housekeeper. "Ms. Fairbearn, who are you really?"

She stared blankly at the Great Bear. "What do you mean, Doctor Bear? I am who I say I am."

"I don't think so. We've checked. *(He didn't mention Ursula.)* Your references are all forgeries. None of the signatories exist. Neither does the employment agency any longer. Dougal, how did you come to use the agency?"

"Her predecessor gave me the name when she left. I dealt with one of the principals."

"Phoebe. Are you really a Canadian? Have you ever been a Chief Housekeeper? I ask again. Who are you really?"

The polar looked up at the ceiling and then the floor. A tear fell from her eye. "All right! I'm a fraud but I needed a job and someplace to disappear. When my cousin left Polar Paradise, we conspired to get me in here. I am an

85

experienced Housekeeper. I am Canadian, but I've lived in Liverpool for the last five years. Now I'm hiding from my mate. He's a gangster and I'm frightened to death of him. He's threatened me any number of times. My real name is Phyllis Phelps. That's my maiden name. My mate's name is Jack DeLad. He's a Grizzly."

A mental bell rang. "Maury, get Fetlock Holmes in here!"

The Horse strode into the conference room. Octavius looked at him and smiled. "Fetlock, meet Jack DeLad's wife. She's hiding from him here. That may explain why you traced him to the Shetlands."

"Oh, please, don't tell him where I am. He wants to kill me. He says I know too much."

"Please come with me, Madam. We need to talk. Don't worry! You'll be safe. Won't she, Bearoness, Octavius?"

The Great Bear shrugged his massive shoulders and looked at Bel. She shrugged back. Neither of them wanted to shove her out the door.

"Phoebe or Phyllis. You can stay on for the moment. Dougal has told us you're doing a very good job. It's probably safer if you don't participate in the pantomime. Too public! We'll get Bearyl to play the part. But we need to talk some more and get some things straightened out if you're going to continue in our employ."

"Oh. Thank you! You won't regret it."

Octavius shrugged again. "I hope not" he muttered.

Belinda looked at him. "Either she's telling the truth or she's one hell of an actress. Let's get Ursula back on her and let's also see what Bearyl thinks.

She needs to chat with her about replacing her in the Momma Bear part. Speaking of which, 'The show must go on.' Can you get the police to free up the theater? Is it a crime scene? Too many guests have signed up for the 'pantos.' I'd hate to disappoint them. We need to keep this very quiet. I don't want a Christmas panic."

I looked at her. "That may be exactly what the Crank has in mind."

Octavius rumbled, "I'll talk to Wardlaw. I also need to find out if they found anything useful with the knives. Are the Cubs OK?"

"It hasn't occurred to them that they might have been hurt or killed. Let's keep it that way. They're still on a high over their first acting jobs. Anyway, Maury, from here on out, watch where you sit!"

"I'm wearing pads under my frilly dress and I'm checking all the props before each performance."

Bearyl came over and said, "If the police will let us, I think we can give this another try in a couple of hours. The stage crew has to re-work the chairs. Maury, I liked what you were doing with the singing. Keep your voice high and childish when you talk. And your tail wagging through the dress is a riot. Octavius, just be your grumpy self. It works fine. We'll just let the Cubs do their thing. The more jumping around they do, the sillier the whole thing looks. I must try on Momma Bear's costume. I hope it fits. I'll just make up some dialogue as we go along."

Chapter Fourteen

Round in circles we're starting to go.

We are really quite anxious to know

If this Preston rings true.

Paul and Paula are who?

Is Ms. Brittany part of his show?

Belinda's smart phone rang. It was the Crank. "Hello Bearoness," said the same disguised voice. "Well, we missed doing in your brats, but we don't discourage easily. The four of you are in our sights. We'll get you. Happy Holidays!"

Condo and Ursula were monitoring all the calls to Bel and Octavius. Once again, this one originated from a windowless basement storage room. They summoned the police and the search was on. The room was bare. No phone! No evidence at all!"

Bruce went ballistic. "Crikey, this time they admitted they were out to kill. This is no Crank. This is a determined murderer or murderers. Who wants you dead? Someone with vengeance on their mind. We need to think this through. What about Dame Bearbi and her son Clarence? They tried to kill you at the Edinbeargh Opera. Where's Chita? She'd know."

(Dame Bearbi Da Savile-Row was the mistress of Bearon Byron Bruin, Belinda's first husband. After being thrown over by the Bearon, she had Clarence set off an avalanche killing him on a ski slope. Then they set about getting revenge on Belinda by trying to kill her. They were thwarted by Colonel Where and Frau Schuylkill. After she and her murderous son had been imprisoned, Chita, who was a junior partner in Bearbi's

publications for females' empire, took over running the magazines, social media sites, TV syndication and marketing activities.)

Ms. Catt was lolling in the Lion and Unicorn lounge polishing off her second dish of champagne. I came out still wearing my Goldilocks' outfit and after putting up with her laughter for a few seconds, got her to join us in the theater. Bruce explained his theory and asked if there were any Da Savile-Row relatives who might have it in for Belinda and her family.

Chita scrunched up her face and replied, "Bearbi has a sister. I've never met her, and she wanted no part of the publications business. Below her aristocratic status 'don't-cha-know.' I don't think there was much love lost between them, but she certainly made it clear she resented the fact that Bearbi and Clarence had the poor breeding to end up in prison for attempted murder. Would she be our Crank? Not out of the question, I suppose, but certainly in bad taste."

"Bearoness, What about your former husband's family?"

Belinda replied, "As far as we know, the ones that are not in prison are back in the Bearents Sea. I'm sure they bear a grudge for being tossed out so unceremoniously and their arrest for their parts in the oil rig sabotage and killings. They were clearly in the employ of *petropol*, the Russian oil conglomerate. Where have I heard that recently?"

"Preston Pavel Polar! Remember Ursula telling us many of his films were funded by the oil combine."

"Right, Maury! Ursula, can you give us some more detail on Preston Pavel Polar and *petropol*?"

89

"Yes, Bearoness. Preston Pavel Polar is related to the Chairbear of *petropol*. His stunt double, Paul, is the Chairbear's son and Preston's cousin. Preston's films have generally been very profitable, and the relationship has been a good one for both parties.

However, Paul and his mate masterminded that infamous set of raids on the Scottish North Sea oil rigs. Due to your team's efforts, that turned out to be a disaster for them. His father did not take kindly to failure and essentially banished Paul and Paula from the company, cancelling their stock holdings and options in the process. They lost heavily as a result. Preston took them on and they have been his stunt doubles for the past year or so. Oddly enough, they are quite skilled in acrobatics, swordplay, gymnastics, explosions, collapses and other near catastrophes."

Chita, who owns a North Sea oil well, willed to her by a rich admirer, said, "You and Octavius blew that phony Bruin family out of the water. Sounds like a pretty good motive for revenge, Bearoness. We thought *petropol* was behind the sabotage of the rigs but could never nail it down. When did the Crank calls begin?"

I said, "I'll check with Dougal, but I think it was about the same time our matinee idol and his entourage arrived."

Octavius was all for facing down the actor and his associates, but Belinda had a different idea. "Let's have another meeting with them, Maury. This time we'll bring Dougal along on the pretext of arranging a facilities tour. Let's see how Paul and Paula react."

When Dougal arrived, Belinda simply told him about the possibility of a film being shot at the Castle and asked him to meet with the actor/producer and his team. Octavius, the Bearoness and I would be there as well. "Oh, by the way, Dougal, when did Preston Pavel Polar arrive at Polar Paradise?"

"Several weeks ago, Milady. He said he needed some time to rest up after his last production and before the holidays. The four of them have been using the pool and have been watching films in the theater. I think they took the jitney ride down to the village."

Meanwhile, I had called the actor and asked if he and his companions could join us for a conference. He was on his way. When he arrived, Brittany was with him but no Paul or Paula. He said they were nursing a pair of hangovers from too much time last night in the Lion and Unicorn lounge.

"Well," I said, "we probably should wait until they're available to have our meeting. After all, they're the ones who will have to decide on what places in the Castle and the grounds you'll need for your 'derring-do.'"

Preston laughed and Brittany dutifully giggled. "You're probably right but I am the one who makes the final decisions. They tell me what is feasible and what is not. I must be careful not to fall into a formula. My fans expect me to do some of their old favorites, but they also insist on seeing new stunts and of course, new love interest." He smiled at Brittany who blushed, giggled again and squeezed his paw.

Belinda smiled and thanked him. "I hope your team is up to enjoying our Aquabear Review and the Christmas Pantomime."

"I'm sure they will be." He rose and the two of them walked back through the lobby.

Octavius strode into the Lion and Unicorn Lounge and called Fiona over. "Fiona, think back about last night. Were the stunt doubles for Preston Pavel Polar in the lounge?"

"Not that I remember, Doctor Bear."

"You don't remember them overdoing their drinking?"

"No Sir. I don't remember seeing them at all. Now, they may have done their drinking somewhere else."

"Or, they may be faking hangovers to avoid us."

"Ursula, do we have any of Preston Pavel Polar's films available?"

"Yes, we do. Which one would you like to see?"

"A recent one that has a lot of stunts and acrobatics. I want to see Paul and Paula in action."

"How about 'Son of the Emperor?' Lots of swordplay and swinging from chandeliers. Or there's 'The Fur'n Legion.' Explosions, scaling walls, diving, gunplay, avalanche and mudslides, damsels in distress."

"Let's see that one. All I want are the action shots. Forget about the love scenes, profiles or arguments. We'll go in one of the conference rooms that has a large screen."

For the next thirty minutes, we were 'treated' to an almost endless parade of perils and rescues, near disasters and super-hyped bravado. Give the cinematographers credit. The transitions from the stars to the stunt doubles were virtually seamless and the costumes and makeup were almost flawless. Brittany was in this one and her screams and horrified expressions were

92

mimicked perfectly by Paula. Laughable as all hell but entertaining nonetheless.

"What are you looking for, Octavius?"

"I just want to see how competent the stunt doubles are. For two people who only recently came on the motion picture scene, they're good. I don't believe there was much CGI or special effects in the dangerous movements. They were doing it themselves. If they are the Cranks, we have a formidable pair to deal with. Let's go back to the theater."

Chapter Fifteen

Octavius has had a close call

He has taken a pretty steep fall.

The Crank's acting faster.

That's one more disaster.

We have got to arrest him, that's all!

The Police finished their scrutiny of the theater, took the stilettos and chairs for analysis and the stage crew substituted two small, breakable seats *(from a seemingly endless supply.)* Bearyl managed to squeeze herself into Momma Bear's dress, put on the gold spectacles and took on a truly amazing matronly look. Octavius simply looked like Octavius. I was back in my now well-padded Goldilocks garb complete with wig and dangling tail. Chita, once again had settled into one of the front seats. The musicians came back and began tuning up and the Twins emerged looking a bit subdued. Belinda and Mlle Woof may have given them a bit of "Instruction." However, the minute they reached the stage, adrenalin and youthful exuberance took over.

Mrs. McRadish, bless her, had come up with a large tureen of highly edible porridge and the crew spilled some into each of the four bowls. The three sets-forest, external house and internal house-were in place. Bearyl was doing double duty as director and Momma Bear. The curtain closed, and she signaled the musicians to start what we called the Four Bears' Theme: a galumphing, repetitive, bass-driven ditty with occasional squeaks to suggest the Baby Bears.

She got herself into the kitchen and the curtain opened partially on the internal set. Momma was spooning out porridge into the bowls and the Twins and Octavius were just about to have their first taste. McTavish took a big gulp, spit it out and yelled. "This porridge is too hot!" Arabella took a dainty bite, scrunched up her nose, dropped her spoon and waving her paws, agreed. Poppa just put his spoon under his nose, turned to Momma and said, "They're right. Let's take a walk in the forest and let it cool down."

The curtain parted further, and they moved through the front door and into the forest, the Cubs jumping and spinning, Poppa shambling and Momma sedately taking mincing steps. After they disappeared stage right, the music changed to my Goldilocks Tra La La skipping song and I bounced and pranced my way out from behind a tree, hopefully inspiring a few laughs with my costume and long protruding tail. I saw the house and capered up to it and wondered if anyone was at home. I looked through the window, turned to the audience and shrugged and tried the front door. It was unlocked. I announced I was hungry. "I smell porridge!" and bounded into the kitchen. I did my "Too hot, too cold, just right!" routine, took the bowl and spoon and headed for the living room. *(OK, here comes the broken chair sequence!)* Admittedly somewhat wary, I tried the big chair, then the medium chair. Neither fit. I gingerly let myself down in one of the Baby chairs. "Just right," I shouted, stood up and the plopped down again with just enough weight and force to break the chair and drop the bowl. I looked at the audience again, shrugged, walked to the stairs and climbed to the next floor.

Yawning emphatically, I spotted the beds and decided a nap was in order. Too hard, too soft, just right! I rolled over and began a high-pitched snore.

At this point, the Bear family returned from their stroll. They walked into the kitchen. It was a real hoot listening to Octavius declaring with rightful indignation. "Someone's been eating my porridge!" followed by a chorus of 'someones' by Momma and the Babies. Arabella picked up her bowl from the floor and cried, "And they ate it all up!" It was then that McTavish discovered that his chair had been destroyed.

They decided to look upstairs for the 'someone.' On the way up on all fours, Octavius slipped and slid all the way down, crashing into Bearyl in the process. The Cubs hadn't started up yet. Arabella screamed, and McTavish jumped back. Bearyl got up, gave the Great Bear a lift with her paws, and shouted for Ian. The musicians stopped. I jumped out of the bed and started down the stairs. Bel and Chita ran up on the stage. There was a stream of oil on the edge of the steps right next to the wall. I had missed it by going up holding the bannister. I took up far less space on the stairs than Octavius. They had to widen them to accommodate him and he used every inch.

Ian was beside himself. "Are ye alright, Doctor Bear? Ms. Bearyl, are ye hurt?" Both signaled they were a bit shook up but otherwise OK. Ian and the crew shouted at each other, pointing paws and casting blame. But, had the Crank struck again? Belinda thought so.

"Oh, this is just too much. We have to track down and stop the Crank(s) immediately or cancel the festivities. I can't have our family, friends, staff and hotel guests all put in jeopardy."

Octavius had sat up and started to get back on his paws while still rubbing his hind leg. "You realize, of course, that would be playing right into the Cranks' paws."

Belinda, clearly upset, came close to screaming. "Well, Genius Crime Fighter, what do you suggest? This place is crawling with law officers, your whole team is here, my staff is at the ready, Ursula is on high alert and we still can't come up with a solution."

"Hangovers or no hangovers, I want to see those stunt doubles immediately. Get the Colonel and Frau Schuylkill to bring them down here, with or without Preston Pavel. Maury, call Inspector Wallaroo and Superintendent Wardlaw to join us."

Mlle Woof took charge of the Cubs and led them off the stage. McTavish rushed over to Octavius and squealed, "Poppa, were you hurt?"

"No, son, Poppa's fine. We're going to have to wait a little while though, before we finish the rehearsal."

Chita and Bearyl took front row seats. Bearyl had a bruise on her hind leg. A 1400-pound Kodiak can be a formidable missile. Ian and his crew were cleaning up the steps and resetting the furniture.

I got on the phone to the two lawmen. Belinda had set the two wolves in motion. Bruce Wallaroo arrived first and after a few Aussie wise cracks about what a bonzer Sheila I made, asked what was going on. I waited till Super Wardlaw arrived and then I played out the Goldilocks Sabotage Scenario #2, followed by our suspicions about the stunt doubles. Ursula filled in the blanks about their previous involvement in the attacks on the North Sea oil rigs.

The wolves returned. The Colonel said, "They're not in their room. Not even sure they're in the hotel. Ilse is checking with Preston Pavel and Brittany right now."

The matinee idol arrived along with the ever-present Brittany. *(She wasn't going to let him out of her sight.)*

Octavius drew himself up to his nine-foot height and rumbled. "Mr. Polar, we have very strong suspicions that your cousin and his mate have been engaged in a series of harassments and dangerous sabotage here at Polar Paradise. We have been trying to find them to question them about a series of so-called accidents that we believe they have initiated in retribution for their losses due to their unsuccessful attacks on Scottish North Sea Oil Rigs. We were responsible for their failures in the North Sea and they may well be getting back at us here at the Castle."

"But this is preposterous, Doctor Bear. Paul and Paula have been with me through several excellent productions. They are dedicated artists and I trust them implicitly. I must. I depend on them not only for their skill but my own personal safety."

The Bear held up his smart phone. "Ursula, will you please enlighten our cinematic guest?"

"Certainly, Doctor Bear. Hello, Mr. Preston Pavel Polar. I am Ursula, UUI Model 7 Artificial Intelligence Unit. We are aware of your and your cousins' connections to *petropol*."

"Of course. I make no secret of that, whoever you are."

"But do you not admit that the reason your cousins are working for you is that they were cut off by your uncle, the Chairbear of *petropol*? They and several Terriers botched a series of attacks on North Sea oil rigs belonging to the Scottish Wildcats. Their failure was primarily the result of discovery and countermeasures by Doctor Bear and his team. We strongly believe with a confidence level of +/- 92% that they are our culprits here at Polar Paradise. We don't know what, if any, involvement you and Miss Brittany have in their activities."

"I don't know what you're talking about, you hysterical computer."

Belinda spoke up. "Preston. I would like nothing better than to accommodate you here at Polar Paradise for your next film. However, I cannot stand idly by and let those Cranks ruin our holiday programs, endanger me and my family and take wanton vengeance on us for uncovering and stopping their deadly North Sea attacks. If you wish, I can have a helicopter here in half an hour and take you and Brittany back to Abeardeen while we seek out your cousin and his mate."

The actor hesitated. He clearly wanted to use the Castle. "Not necessary, Bearoness. I will call them, and we will clear up this slander. I know nothing about North Sea oil rigs and I'm sure neither do they. Your Artificial Intelligence unit is wildly off base." He stalked off with Brittany.

"Well, he's certainly a convincing actor, isn't he?" I said, "But one thing is bothering me. If Paul and Paula are our Cranks, how do they know so much about this castle?"

Frau Ilse snarled, "They have help! Probably one of those verdammt Pipers."

Chapter Sixteen

Three Bagpipers emerge from the past.

Are they back to get even at last?

They were chased once before.

So, to even the score

Did they set up the Christmas Tree blast?

The Frau was referring to the four *(now three)* terrier Castle Pipers who turned out to be the villains in the oil rig sabotage. *(See Book Three - The Case of Scotch)* Using a phony Royal Environmental Protection Authority boat stored in the base of the Castle, Jock, Trevor, Angus and auld Robbie, now deceased, would conduct random inspections of oil rigs. These were shortly followed by some form of disaster -fires, broken lines, scuttled support boats, damaged helicopters. Several of the oil platform workers were wounded, maimed or killed in the process. When the Terriers and the boat were discovered by Octavius and his group, they took off in an unmarked helicopter. They had never been paid by the Bruin family (or to use their actual identities, the Bearents Polars in the employ of *petropol's* agents, Paul and Paula.) The Terriers knew the castle and its many hidden rooms from top to bottom.

Ursula had tracked Jock and Trevor to locations in England and Angus to the south of France. Were any of them now here at Polar Paradise? Had they returned to collect their back wages from Paul and Paula and wreak revenge on the Bearoness and her family, friends and the Castle? It seemed increasingly likely.

Frau Ilse tried her theory out on Inspector Wardlaw and the rest of us. Ursula calculated the probabilities as extremely high. We agreed. Now, were we talking about one or all three of the conspirators?

Belinda's smart phone rang. This time, the Crank had a different voice. Was it Scottish? "Holiday Greetings! So, you aristocratic bitch! You've found us out. But can you find us? It won't be easy and meanwhile you and your minions are in for a very rough ride. By the way, Preston, that egotistical jerk, has tried to get us to give ourselves up. Not likely! He and that stupid sow, Brittany are going to have to do their own stunts. Isn't that a hoot. Catch us if you can! Bye-bye for now but not for long!"

I briefly ruminated. "Was that a Piper or was it Paul? It could have been Preston. After all, he is the actor. He can change voices, inflections and pacing. Maybe he's trying to cast suspicion on his cousins. Or maybe not. Maybe I'm going paranoid along with everyone else. I don't trust any of them."

Belinda looked at me. "Thanks for helping to clarify things, Maury. Does Preston also have some kind of grievance against us? Is this whole thing a massive tail-chasing exercise? My frustration level is reaching its limits. Get Dougal in here!"

When the sheepdog arrived, Belinda was beginning to cool off. "Dougal, we have reason to believe that one or more of the three Terrier Pipers who escaped from the Castle after being revealed as the oil rig saboteurs, may be back here in Polar Paradise. Jock or Trevor or Angus! We think he or they may be involved along with Paul and Paula in the so-called accidents we've been sustaining. I want him or them found. I want you to lead the police and members of our team, the Wolves and Otto, in searching out every nook and cranny of this Castle. If it is them, they know this place upside down. So do you. Find him or them. Turn some of your management duties over to Ms. Fairbearn temporarily. Incidentally, where is she?"

Dougal replied, "Last I saw of her, she was with the detective, Fetlock Holmes. I'll find her and send her to ye. Meanwhile, Milady, we'll start the search. I remember those three vera, vera well."

Dougal turned to the members of Shetland Yard along with the Wolves and Otto. "Would ye please come with me so we can organize this hunt. We'll have to be careful not to disturb the paying guests. I think we should start in some of the storage and utility areas. I'll take ye to the outside lift that connects a roof parapet with the dock down below the cliffs. It also has a couple of stops in between. The Pipers used it when they went out on their raids in the camouflaged environmental boat. They could move about without being in the occupied parts of the building."

Several minutes later, Phoebe Fairburn (aka Phyllis Phelps) arrived, accompanied by Fetlock Holmes. The Horse neighed and said, "Superintendent Wardlaw, we have located Jack DeLad. He is holed up in a cottage near Baltasound. I need your assistance in taking him captive. He is armed and dangerous. I doubt he will surrender without a battle. Ms. Phelps has been most obliging in helping us locate him. For her own safety, she should stay here at the Castle."

This put Wardlaw in a bit of a dilemma. What should be his priority? Use his resources to capture a wanted criminal or help search out the Polar Paradise Crank. He looked at Octavius. "Doctor Bear, I believe my duty lies in capturing Jack DeLad. We have been searching for him for a long time and as Fetlock Holmes says. 'He is armed and dangerous.' I believe you have sufficient resources among your own team to initiate a search for the Cranks. We will return to assist you as rapidly as we can."

Octavius and Belinda weren't happy but couldn't deny the Collie's logic. The Bearoness offered one of the Polar Paradise helicopters to supplement the Shetland Yard vehicles.

"That is most generous of you, Bearoness. Thank you!"

"Just partially repaying some long-standing debts, Superintendent."

Octavius called for Dougal and explained the situation. "Bruce, can you, Condo and Chita help Dougal in our search. I have released Ursula from her constraints. Take the Flying Tigers, too. They can assist. With Otto and the Wolves, we should be able to scour the Castle."

Belinda went over to Ms. Fairbearn. "Phoebe, or is it Phyllis?"

"The staff know me as Phoebe Fairbearn, Milady. Let's avoid confusion and stick with that."

"Fine, Phoebe! You are going to have to take over some of Dougal's responsibilities while he and our team are tracking down our persecutors. I know you are not as familiar as he is with the Castle and the properties."

"I'm a quick learner, Milady and I am so grateful to you for keeping me on."

"OK! Get with Dougal before he leads his safari. Bearyl has taken your place as Momma Bear if we ever get the pantomime off the ground. You'll have to supervise the Christmas Eve choristers. We have about a dozen fine voices among the staff. I believe Mrs. McRadish has been taking the time to rehearse them."

"You'll also need to complete the arrangements for temporary personnel on Boxing Day when many of our permanent employees will have the day off to go home and celebrate. We need to have a brief ceremony to give them their holiday gifts. AND we must contend with these Crank nut cases, so for God's sake, be careful. Still want to stay on?"

"Yes, Milady, after years of living with Jack DeLad, I'm not afraid of anything."

"You may want to think twice about that statement but go find Dougal."

Out in the courtyard a Police helicopter and a Polar Paradise utility chopper with Fetlock Holmes aboard took off for the short journey to Baltasound and the face-off with Jack DeLad. On the way, Super Wardlaw had an idea. He told the pilot to let them down next to the Lion and Unicorn Pub. Those two worthies emerged from the bar and strode over to the whirlybird.

"Och," Said Lion, "What brings the Police to our establishment, Superintendent? We've not been pouring unlicensed brew or serving underage animals."

"No, Lion, I need a favor. Can you still shatter windows with your roar?"

"Aye and my horned partner is pretty good at stomping up a thundering drum."

"Wonderful, we have a villain Grizzly Bear named Jack DeLad cornered in a nearby cottage and he won't come out. He's dangerous but we want him alive. We could use a powerful amount of noise to shake him up."

The two of them laughed. *(An ominous sound in itself)* Lead on, Superintendent. Who's the Horse in that other helicopter?"

"That's Consulting Detective Fetlock Holmes. He tracked him down."

"Well, let's have at this Grizzly."

The Collie moved up near the cottage. "Jack DeLad, this is Shetland Yard. We have you surrounded. Surrender peacefully and things will go more easily for you."

The Grizzly fired a gun in the Super's direction. "No surrender, Copper," he growled.

That was the signal for Lion and Unicorn to create a thundering roar, shattering the windows of the cottage and sending the Grizzly into paroxysms of pain. As he was convulsing, the Scotland Yard sergeants rushed him and wrestled him to the ground. They hit him with a taser and cuffed his front and back paws.

Fetlock Holmes let out a neigh of approval. "Quite Satisfactory! I didn't realize you had a secret weapon, Superintendent."

"Yes, those two can be quite formidable, Mr. Holmes. I have seen them use a greatly reduced version to get some unruly drinkers back in line. I think you saw them at maximum strength today. Lion, Unicorn, thanks for your assistance. Unfortunately, I'm on duty but you may want to offer some of your wares to Fetlock Holmes, here."

The horse came over and shook hooves and paws with the two pub owners and allowed as how he hadn't tasted a true single malt Scotch in quite a while. While the sergeants hauled the Grizzly into the police helicopter and left for Abeardeen, Wardlaw and Holmes headed for the hostelry.

The place was filled with tourists down from the Castle. They had not expected the excitement of an authentic police capture and were on their smart phones taking pictures and sending messages. Fetlock Holmes had his Scotch and Superintendent Wardlaw, conscious of the audience, made do with a lemonade. They bade everyone goodbye, headed for the Castle helicopter and took off back to Polar Paradise.

Chapter Seventeen

AI Ursula's changes were swift

To the codes on the external lift.

And she's crippled the pumps.

The Crank's down in the dumps

His escape route's been given short shrift.

Back at Polar Paradise: The Castle search began. Dougal and our team took an internal lift *(elevator)* to the roof and proceeded to the parapet facing the bay. "The military installed this external lift during the Great War to bring up weapons and radar to the Castle roof but they werena' put to use. The war ended too soon. The lift descends outside the cliff face to a dock below."

"After decommissioning and removing the military hardware and turning the Castle back to the Bruin family, the lift was kept in place. There are several stops in the shaft leading to utility areas and one that opens on the theater. The young Bearon used it to secretly enter and exit the Castle. We believe he was engaged in smuggling as well as bringing in 'friends', if ye get my meaning."

"Somehow, the Pipers got the combination to the controls and used it when they went on their oil rig raiding parties. If one or more of them is hiding here, they're likely to be somewhere with entrances to the shaft. Ye'll also notice that it gives access to the theater where some of the recent attacks have taken place."

Otto piped up, "Let's test the lift. When we were chasing the Pipers the last time, the doors opened in the parapet on an empty shaft. Then I got stranded between floors and left to die. I zapped out. This thing can be a fearsome weapon."

Members of the team recalled what had happened. This seemed like a job for Ursula. Colonel Where called on the AI System. "Ursula, can you change the coding on the lift controls? We don't know whether or not our opponents can use the elevator but let's make sure they can't."

"Certainly, Colonel Where. I've wiped out the access codes and replaced them with a 1024 public and private crypto key and algorithm. Let's test it."

The parapet door opened and sure enough, no car. A whining sound and the cables started spinning. A pair of interior doors appeared and opened. "OK, let's send it down to the bottom."

The car doors closed, and the parapet entrance shut. More whining "Where is it now?"

"Approaching the bottom. It's an eleven-story drop. It's built to carry heavy loads, not super speed. OK, it's down."

Otto squeaked again. "Dougal, did they dismantle the sea flood mechanisms down at the dock. We were almost drowned by a deluge pumped up at the platform. Chita rescued us."

"I honestly don't know, Mr. Otter."

Ursula once more interceded. "The pumps are still there, Otto. I can alter the controls on them. We may want to use them if the Pipers are trying to escape again. Assuming, of course, that they are here."

Condo had a thought. "Please do that, Ursula. Let's call up Harold and see what he knows about the pumps and the natural tides. Is it safe to go down there?"

Harold, the sea otter, is in charge of the water sports, sea conditions, beaches and vessels in use at the Polar Paradise. He has the tidal tables memorized and tightly controlled.

He responded to a smart phone call. "Aye, there are two boats down at the hidden dock. A Zodiac and a Whaler. They're inside a pair of sealed compartments to keep out the water. Right now, there are two more hours before the tide comes in. We have crippled the undersea pumps by scrambling the infra-red controls, but they can be re-activated. Right now, it's safe to be on the dock. I'll meet ye all there."

Chita decided that her life-long distaste for water was going to keep her on the roof until we began our searches. The Flying Tigers had no such feline issues. They still lived in wonder at what they had signed on for with Octavius and the Bearoness. Never a dull moment.

Checking one more time with Ursula, we crowded into the lift car and headed for the bottom. As we descended, we made note of the four intermediate stops. Ursula had altered their entry and exit codes as well. We would split up and take on each of those floors after checking out the dock. If the Pipers and *petropol* polars intended to use the lift, they were in for a serious disappointment.

We met Harold on the platform. He opened the compartments containing the Zodiac and Whaler. The Zodiac showed signs of recent use. I asked, "Harold, any idea who took the Zodiac out?"

"Nae, Mr. Meerkat. Nobody has signed it out. The winter seas are a bit rough for most amateur sailors to say nothin' of the cold. An outboard Zodiac would get bumped around pretty sharpish. I dinna ken who would take it, sail it and bring it back. More than one animal, for certain."

"Ok, we want you to seal the compartments and change the codes on the door locks. We don't want anyone to have access to those boats."

"Aye! Is there a problem?"

"We're not sure. We're searching for the animals who have been causing all the grief around the Castle and we want to deny them the use of the lift, the dock and the boats. They may or may not be using them, but they won't be able to now."

Inspector Wallaroo turned to Dougal. "Does the household staff use this lift for anything?"

"Aye, we move heavy furniture and such that won't fit in the internal lifts."

"If anyone needs to use it, have them call you and we'll open it up for them. Now, let's break out into teams and start searching for our unwelcome guests."

They split into 3 groups:

1. Otto; Frau Ilse; Colonel Where
2. Dougal; Condo; Chita
3. Bruce; Ben and Gal (The Flying Tigers)

Each group had an Ursula subsystem in hand and at least one weapon. We decided to leave the theater till last to allow one more try at rehearsing the pantomime.

I returned to the panto troupe, donning my well-padded Goldilocks costume. The stage crew had scrubbed down the stairway and were checking out the scenery. One of the wheels on the rotating internal house flat had broken off. Not sure whether that was an accident or more sabotage. Bearyl called the cast together including the Cubs and Octavius and gave us some director's notes. The musicians were back and once again, tuning up. More porridge arrived from the kitchen. The chairs were tested. Showtime!!

Miracle of miracles! We got all the way through and as I went screaming out into the forest followed by a galumphing Poppa Bear and closing music, we all breathed a major sigh of relief. *(Exit pursued by a bear.)* The Cubs wanted to do it again. Bearyl decided to leave well enough alone. Belinda declared victory and went out to hunt down Ms. Fairbearn to go over the preparations for Christmas Eve.

In addition to supervising the Polar Paradise kitchens, whipping up porridge for the pantomime and getting the staff replacing the Boxing Day celebrants assigned and clued in, Mrs. McRadish took time to rehearse the Christmas Eve choristers. What a marvelous sheep!

Belinda was especially worried that the Crank(s) would undermine the kitchens. She called together the chefs and sous-chefs, the maître-d's, wait staff, Mrs. McRadish and Ms. Fairbearn. She also called in Fiona from the Lion and Unicorn Lounge. "Ladies and Gentlebeasts. As you know, we are being subjected to some intense harassment by unknown animals who are clearly intent on wreaking havoc on Polar Paradise over the holidays."

"We are dedicated to stopping their efforts and bringing them to judgement. Our food and drink services are outstanding and have, in the short time we have been open, won several major awards. That makes us a very inviting target for these reprobates."

"I need every one of you to take extreme care in the preparation and service of our meals and beverages. If you even suspect someone has tampered with the food, drinks or dining room amenities and ambience, you are to report it immediately to Mrs. McRadish, Ms. Fairbearn or me. Dougal is currently carrying out a critical assignment for us and will not be available. But we will."

"Anyone caught meddling in any way with our food and drinks service will be dealt with summarily, including being turned over to the police. I'm sorry to be so strict, especially during the holidays, but this is a critical situation. I hope we can clear this up shortly and allow all of us to enjoy Christmas, Boxing Day and New Year's Day. Thank you!" Her phone rang. Same Crank voice. "What a wonderful speech, Bearoness. Do you really believe you can track us down? Lots of Luck!"

Chapter Eighteen

We are on the utility floor

Where the Cranks practiced mischief galore.

They installed a black box

And they altered keylocks

And we're trying to find if there's more.

I rejoined the Crank Hunters Team 3 - Bruce and the Flying Tigers. They were on the utility floor right above the dock. It's an open space broken only by support pillars. Two staircases on opposite ends of the floor led up to the next level. No steps going down to the dock. A large indoor lift ran along an interior wall. Along another wall sat a series of generators and furnace/air conditioner units connected, no doubt, to compressors on the roof and ducts throughout the building.

A large electrical distribution panel studded with circuit breakers dominated the center of the floor with a mass of cables emerging into the ceiling. Another large, glassed-in unit housed the communications center supplying front desk, phone, internet, TV and room access services. The electronic guest room keylocks were controlled from here. A small office housed the duty technician who was somewhat taken aback by the sudden appearance of our group.

He stepped out and shouted, "Ye should not be down here. This is a highly restricted area."

Bruce replied, "We know. This is a search authorized by the Bearoness and Dougal. I'm Chief Inspector Bruce Wallaroo of the Australian Police. This is Mr. Mauritius Meerkat, Doctor Octavius Bear's Executive Assistant and these two white Tigers are assisting us in tracking down several individuals that we believe are trying to sabotage the Castle. Get on your phone and call either Dougal or the Bearoness. We'll stand here while you do."

While he was calling, I turned around and looked at the doors to the external lift from which we had just emerged. They were painted a functional grey to match most of the other equipment and just seemed to be another large closet. Good camouflage!

The technician was conversing with Dougal, and he came over, held out the phone and said, "Mr. Dougal wants to talk with ye. He wants to make sure ye're who ye say ye are."

I spoke briefly to the Sheepdog and handed the phone back to the technician. He listened, shook his head affirmatively, shrugged and said, "I guess it's awright! Mr. Dougal says to give ye a hand. What can I do fer ye?"

"Over the last several weeks, has anyone been down here who isn't part of your regular rotation?"

"Let me look at the log. Last week, there were two polar bears working on the guest room keylock system. They had proper ID and were here for about two hours. They said that some of the locks weren't responding to the guests' keycards. We also had two terriers upgrading several of the internet servers. They had proper ID. Routine maintenance, they called it. They keep spare parts in that closet over there. That's it."

"Did you recognize any of them. Had they been here before?"

"Now that ye mention it, they weren't the usual technicians. They said they were substituting for the customary teams who were away for the holidays."

114

Bruce took up his phone and called the Condor. "Condo? Bruce Wallaroo! We need you down here on the utility deck. I think there's been some tampering with the keylock system and the internet servers. Two Polar Bears and Two Terriers. Sound suspicious? I think so too! Fine! Tell Dougal. An Ursula is with us and she is doing diagnostics on the systems as we speak. We'll be waiting."

It turns out that the floor Dougal, Condo and Chita were inspecting was empty. It is normally used to store spare dining and conference room furniture. but all of its contents had been pressed into service for the holiday events. Two staircases and an internal lift matched the ones on the utility deck. Once again, the external lift doors were disguised as large closets. All three decided to join us below.

Condo arrived and conferred with Ursula. They then examined the keylock system. "It looks like our "friends" have set ten rooms to permanent unlocked status. That's probably where they hide between their raids. Are Superintendent Wardlaw and his sergeants back yet?"

I responded, "I'll call him and check his whereabouts."

Chapter Nineteen

Here we go! Once again it is time

To put on the bear pantomime.

There's another strange dish;

A lost kettle of fish

In the kitchen. Is that a Crank crime?

"Wardlaw here! Hello, Maury. We just sent a tasered and tied up Jack DeLad down to Abeardeen accompanied by Sergeant Drummond. Sergeant McRuff, Fetlock Holmes and I are coming back to the Castle on the Bearoness' utility helicopter. Any news of our Cranks?"

I told him about our discoveries. The keylocks to Rooms 90 through 99 have been put on constant unlock by two polar bears. I asked him to join us in the corridor for those rooms.   Two terriers have been working on the internet servers. Condo and Ursula are checking the servers out. Not sure what mischief they will uncover.

We all took up positions in the corridor leading to Rooms 90 through 99 while we waited for Superintendent Wardlaw. The front desk assured us those rooms were empty. We knew better. When the Collie and his sergeant arrived, we proceeded to open the unlocked doors of each room. Guess who we found in Room 95. The Terriers Jock and Trevor were asleep but not for long. Wardlaw and Sergeant McRuff rushed into the room. "Jock and Trevor! You are under arrest. You have the right to keep silent, but anything you do say will be recorded and may be used against you."

Trevor reached under his pillow and pulled out a pistol. Condo slammed it out of his paw. Chita jumped on him and the Superintendent wrestled Jock to the floor. Sergeant McRuff cuffed them both.

Wardlaw continued. "We are not certain what you and your co-conspirators plan next for damaging the Polar Paradise, but we have had warrants out for your arrest since you escaped after sabotaging the Scottish North Sea oil rigs. That will be enough for us to bring you before the bench. As our investigations here progress, we'll have more evidence to charge you with harassment, willful damage, attempted murder and conspiring to injure or kill members of the Bear family as well as their staff, employees and guests. You also pulled a weapon on members of Her Majesty's constabulary. Not looking very good for you or smart."

Jock barked back, "You can't prove a thing, you stupid cop!"

Wardlaw grinned, "Try us. Now, who are you working with?"

Trevor whined, "Nobody. We deny everything. We don't have any partners."

"We'll see how long you stick with that story. All right Sergeant, let's get them down to Abeardeen. Could several of you give the Sergeant a hand. We'll have to use the Bearoness' helicopter. He turned to me and Fetlock Holmes. "It's been a busy day, but I doubt this is over yet."

Truer words were never spoken. Bruce and the Flying Tigers picked up the Terriers bodily and hauled them out to the helicopter. Ben volunteered to fly the chopper, leaving the Shetland Yard pilot to support Super Wardlaw. Sergeant McRuff kept the ex-Pipers subdued as they headed for the Abeardeen Gaol.

The rest of us searched each one of the unlocked rooms. If the Crank Polars had been in any of them, they had scarpered while we were taking down the Terriers. Condo went down to the utility deck and restored the rooms to the locked condition. One less area for the Cranks to hide.

It turned out that the Terriers had also hacked into the hotel security camera system. They and the Cranks could watch the entire premises from their rooms and shut the system down, if they wanted to. One more restoration job for Condo and Ursula.

I called Octavius and Belinda and brought them up to speed. They congratulated us but agreed that we still needed to find the real Cranks. They had lost their confederates and needed new hiding places, but we couldn't rely on them being slowed down for long.

Sure enough, Belinda's phone rang again. "Hello, Bearoness! Well, points to your side but the game is still ours. It's Christmas Eve. Got some presents for you. Jingle bells!"

Belinda was seething. "I suppose I should be happy that the Aquashows have gone off well with no further damage. The pantomime starts in half an hour and we have it well checked out and guarded. The Christmas tree is still intact and now those two dogs are in custody. But I want those two, if there are two, Cranks strung up. I hope the police can get those Terriers to talk."

Octavius was in the theater and Mlle Woof had just brought the two Cubs down for their performance. I was running down to get into my Goldilocks costume and Bearyl was going over last-minute details, first with the musicians and then with the stage crew. Ian had just completed a thorough check of the scenery and props for the third time that day.

Chita was once again in the front row. Superintendent Wardlaw and the Shetland Yard pilot; Fetlock Holmes; Chief Inspector Wallaroo and the Wolves took up places around the theater. Otto and Belinda had just come from the matinee Aquabears performance. Gal of the Flying Tigers sat down next to Chita-two formidable felines. Ben was still on his run to Abeardeen. Condo was perched up on a light-tower and was once again conferring with Ursula. The audience started to trickle in with shouts, laughs and occasional cries from the juvenile members. The Frau and Colonel were keeping a special watch for any suspicious looking characters.

Lo and behold, coming through the door and taking up seats in the center section were Preston Pavel Polar, Brittany AND Paul and Paula. Belinda spotted them and jerked to attention. She slowly walked over to Superintendent Wardlaw and pointed them out. Since they had no reason other than strong suspicion, the policeman could really do nothing except keep a constant watch on them. She sent a text message to Octavius who relayed it to me. All four of them were there.

Bel then walked over to the actor and his entourage, thanked them for coming and asked them not to be too critical of the performances. Pantomimes were supposed to be ridiculous and slapstick. They would get that in abundance. Brittany giggled loudly, and Preston said something reassuring with a broad smile on his snout. Paul and Paula just nodded.

Backstage, Octavius and I noted their presence. "What do you think?" I asked, "Trying to throw us off?"

"We can't prove anything and there's a slim chance we might be wrong. There were certainly two polars involved in tampering with the keylocks, but this Castle is crawling with polars. We have plenty of support out in the theater in case they do try something, but I have a strong suspicion they are just giving us the bird. Meanwhile, we have some silliness to attend to."

And we did! The Cubs refused the porridge; the bears went for a walk; I skipped and "tra-la-ed," ate porridge and broke the chair; went upstairs and fell asleep. The bears returned; bemoaned the eaten porridge and the broken chair; caught me in the bed and sent me screaming out into the forest. End of Pantomime. Roars of Laughter as only polars can roar. Standing Ovation. Special bows for the Cubs. Special bow from Bearyl. Special curtsey from me with my long tail sticking out from my dress. House lights up and on to refreshments and Boxing Day.

Preston, his suave self in high gear, came over and congratulated Belinda. He waited till the Cubs appeared and shook both of their paws. Brittany gave them a hug. Paul and Paula had disappeared.

I had taken off my costume and walked over to Ian who was talking to Bearyl. "Will the same crew be on hand for the Boxing Day performance?"

"Aye, Mr. Meerkat. We're giving them the day off after Boxing Day. They're all satisfied with that. And there is no Christmas performance so several of them will be away from the Castle tomorrow. As long as those mischief-makers are still at large, we'll give the theater a complete shakedown on Boxing Day morning."

"Great," said Bearyl. "Thanks again for your excellent work on today's performance, Ian. You guys are true professionals. The audience loved it."

"You are very welcome, Ms. Bearyl. 'Tis a fun show to do. I'm bringing my wife and our two bairns to the Boxing Day program. They always wonder what their auld Dad does for a livin'."

Out in the theater, Belinda's phone rang again. This time it was Mrs. McRadish. "Sorry to disturb ye, Milady. But we've had a spot of trouble here in the kitchens. Several kettles of fish are missing and so are two of the new wait staff we brought on for the holidays. We can work around it, but I thought ye'd like to know."

Octavius had shambled over. "Well done, Poppa Bear. You have a new career ahead of you if you want it."

"Sorry, Bel, show biz is your specialty. I have enough on my plate."

"Speaking of plates, Mrs. McRadish just called. We have a mystery on our paws in the kitchens. We…" Her phone rang again.

"Hello Bearoness! *(The Crank)* Well, isn't that a fine kettle of fish for Christmas Eve. Just wanted you to know we're still around. We're sorry to lose the Terriers but that's the breaks."

"Ursula, did you get a lock on that call?"

"Yes, Bearoness. This time it came from outside the building. The last one came from a hallway in one of the guest wings. They're moving around."

"Tavi, they're playing with us. One annoyance after another."

"Maybe, Bel, but I think it's more than just being a nuisance. It's a cat and mouse game but remember, in the end, the cat usually kills the mouse. We need to get rid of them permanently and quickly."

"Well, we've cut off some of their flexibility. They can't use the external lift or the boats down in the dock. The security cameras are back on line and behaving as they should. They can't use the rooms they had unlocked, and the Terriers are penned up in Abeardeen. We outnumber them. We have Ursula and Otto and Condo and the Wolves, to say nothing of the Shetland and Australian Police. Then there's Maury, Bearyl, Chita, Jake and Lepi, The Flying Tigers, you and me. I'm tired of waiting for the next shoe to drop. *(If they're wearing shoes.)* I don't want to upset our guests or spoil the holidays, but I think we have to get more aggressive."

"OK, what do you have in mind?"

"For openers, let's free up Ursula from her 'harm restrictions', if you haven't already. You saw how she handled those fire-bombing birds." *(See Book Seven-The Suit Case)*

"She's not in restrained mode."

"Good! Ursula, can you track and eliminate the Cranks?"

"I will need more data, Bearoness. The calls have been too short to lock on to the caller. However, I have been analyzing pawprints at the attack scenes. Many of them belong to the Terriers but there are also a few polar bear prints. One set has a split in the right front pad."

"Can you check where the Preston Pavel Polar party was seated in the theater?"

"Unfortunately, the cleaning crew has been through the theater, vacuuming the floors and wiping down the seats. Nothing definitive but I will track Preston and his crew."

Chapter Twenty

The Calendar says Christmas Day

And Santa's long gone on his way.

He's left all sorts of toys

For the good girls and boys.

Have the Cranks left? It's too soon to say.

We had changed the Christmas Eve program for the Choristers. Instead of wandering the halls, they would begin singing in the lobby and then move to the dining rooms during the dinner hour. There were ten in all under Mrs. McRadish's direction.

With the exception of the purloined fish, Christmas Eve dinner came off without a hitch. Oh, there was the occasional drunk who had too much wassail and the juvenile who had a talent for spilling things, but all told, things went well. Dougal, Ms. Fairbearn and Mrs. McRadish bustled about smoothing things out.

The kitchens were at high fever pitch, but efficient service was maintained. Belinda and Octavius cruised through the dining rooms, wishing each table Season's Greetings and accepting the congratulations of the guests. The choristers managed to get some of the more extroverted animals to join in the singing and an impromptu dance recital broke out among four Red Foxes. I drew the line at wearing my Goldilocks outfit. Somehow, Mlle Woof managed to keep the Cubs under control. *(McTavish wanted to order porridge.)*

Chita, Otto, the Wolves, Flying Tigers, Bearyl, Bearnice, Lepi, Jake, Condo, Bruce and I all retired to the Lion and Unicorn Lounge and toasted the transition at midnight to Christmas Day. Ursula joined us, Doctors 'Odd' Vark and Chiti had come down from the Clinic for dinner and we called Howard and Marlin back in Cincinnati without regard to time zone differences. *(The electrons were still feverishly coupling.)* Not quite sure where the police or Fetlock Holmes had disappeared to. Speaking of disappearances, Preston and his party were nowhere to be seen. Finally, Belinda and Octavius joined us and relaxed. "Merry Christmas, all!"

Wonder of wonders! No Crank calls!

Christmas morning. Belinda talked Octavius into wearing a Santa Claus outfit (or at least a red hat and top) and bringing out presents for the Cubs in front of a smaller Christmas tree in the family suite. Two space suits with plexiglass helmets and embroidered names; two rocket-shaped, electric wagons; a large and detailed launch and control system courtesy of Ursula and tons of other stuff. I got a carefully wrapped bowl of porridge. Frau Schuylkill presented Octavius with a crystal keg of Lion and Unicorn's vintage mead. The Bearoness got a lovely blue sapphire from Octavius, smaller than the infamous Deep Blue *(See Book One- The Open and Shut Case)* but still dazzling.

The Aquabears will be performing twice today at a matinee and evening show. Otto will be dressed as an Elf and do a few very special capers.

At lunch, the staff will gather in one of the dining rooms to receive their Boxing Day gifts from "Santa" Octavius and "Mrs. Santa" Belinda. All the wrapped gifts were carefully opened, scanned and rewrapped. Four contained dead mice. The Crank was at it again. Thank goodness there was nothing deadlier. The gifts were then stored in a large utility closet under lock and key plus a rotating shift of guards. After the lunch-time gathering, the departing staff can start their holiday early. The dining rooms will be reduced to two and buffets will be available for lunch and evening meals. The same will hold true for Boxing Day where the main feature will be a repeat of the Goldilocks pantomime. Tra-la-la!

Bearnice, Lepi, Chita and Jake have been rehearsing on and off for their New Year's Eve performance. Bearnice and Lepi were well on their way to becoming singing sensations. Bearyl was also going to do a couple of selections from her dramatic monologue series that had her booked solidly through next year. As their agent, I was of course, delighted.

Lepi and Jake came over to me. Jake said, "Hey, Goldilocks! What's the story with this Crank or Cranks? We haven't been involved till now, but we are crazy about the Bearoness and want to help her out as best we can."

Lepi shook his noble head in agreement. A Himalayan Snow Leopard and a Jaguar can make up a formidable team and these guys were not prissy artistic pussy cats. Add Chita and the Polar Twins to the mix and you have some serious "fire power."

I sat them down with a couple of drinks and took them through the "History of the Crazy Cranks."

Leperello blinked and exclaimed, "It's been a while since I was a member of the Chinese Peoples' Guard, but I haven't lost any of my martial skills. Sounds like those terriers were only half the story. Jake and I want to meet Ursula. She can help us plan out our parts in this extravaganza. What's your take on Preston Pavel Productions?"

"I don't trust them, but we have no real proof."

"Should we try to cozy up to them? I've always wanted to be in pictures and both of us are pretty exotic characters."

"Sounds good to me. Let's get together with Ursula. She can give you some in-depth background and suggestions. I'll call her up for you. Ursula!"

"Yes, Goldi…Sorry, Mr. Meerkat."

I knew I was going to regret taking that part. "Have you met my two good friends, Jake the Jaguar and Leperello the Himalayan Snow Leopard?"

"No, I haven't but I know all about them."

"Gentlebeasts, you have to get used to a Universal Ursine Intellect – Artificial General Intelligence Model 7. She knows more than you know, and she knows before you know, but she is extremely valuable to have around. Ursula, what's the best way to get these two cats together with Preston Pavel?"

"Just a suggestion! Preston Pavel has never had to contend with fierce felines in any of his pictures. You two would make ideal villains for the great matinee idol to take on. That, of course, is if you're willing to play bad guys. Perhaps, Mr. Meerkat, you would like to put on your agent's sunglasses and introduce your two latest clients: Jake the Javelin and Lepi the Leveler."

The two cats fell into a spasm of laughter; gave each other high fives; slapped me on the back and howled. "Maybe we should bring in Chita as our 'moll.' Wonderful, Ursula, just wonderful!"

Picking myself up from the floor, I agreed. "I'll tell the Bearoness first and then we'll 'take a meeting' with Preston. Let's include Chita but let's hold Bearyl and Bearnice in reserve. He may have too many Polar Bears already and Brittany may get jealous."

I went off to track down the Bearoness and Chita. Belinda was all for holding the session. Ms. Catt allowed as how she had not played a ne'er-do-well since her days with Imperius Drake. "It will be a fun exercise!"

I phoned Octavius and got him on board. I called Preston's suite and actually reached him. I explained that there were a few introductions I wanted to make and gave him a brief view of our "Feline Felons" proposal. He was interested, and we agreed to meet in a conference room in half an hour.

Ursula was monitoring all this in the background. She had done a Deep Data plunge and came out with a 'Bad Uns' composite to pass on to the cats. Arrest history, convictions, personal tics, *(Ever seen a jaguar tossing a silver dollar with his tail?)* snarls, accents, growls and roars. Lepi knew how to handle a gun. Jake didn't. Chita got a whole new set of struts, wiggles, perfume and cheap jewelry. She was also chewing gum. On to the audition.

Belinda joined us for a few minutes before heading off to the pool to prepare for the matinee performance of the Aquabears' Christmas Revue. Otto stopped in, decked out in his green and white elf outfit.

Preston Pavel Polar and Brittany arrived and there were paw shakes all around. The Cats fell into character immediately with Jake threatening Brittany; Lepi warning Preston to stay out of his territory, all the while keeping Chita on his front paw. Preston got into the mood and showing a major case of attitude, faced down the Snow Leopard. Roars, snarls, pushes and shoves. Chita ran over to Brittany and swatted at her with her paw. *(Missing her, of course!)* Suddenly, the movie star broke out in gusts of laughter.

"Well," he gasped, "that's certainly something new. Most of my films thus far have been Bears vs. Bears or the occasional Wolf. Now, we have the

Fearsome Felines. I like it. It's different and you guys are certainly authentic criminals." *(Little did he know about Chita and Imperius Drake!)*

Ever the opportunistic agent, I chimed in, "We have a couple of pretty scary Wolves and a pair of white Bengal Tigers you might also want to meet." *(I wasn't sure how the Frau and the Colonel would react to being cast as criminals in a 'potboiler' and I'm not sure whether Ben and Gal could act to save themselves. But what the Hell!)*

"You've given me a lot to think about, Maury." *(Exactly what we had in mind, Preston. If you really are the Crank, we have some formidable folks for you to contend with. Thought we'd give you a sample.)*

Brittany seemed a bit shocked. The Cats could certainly trigger her 'damsel in distress' reactions. *(Again, a kind of warning shot. We hadn't figured her out yet. Could she be a Crank?)*

I don't really know what we had just accomplished besides giving the Cats a chance to enjoy themselves. They all called out Ursula and congratulated her on her strategy. I think I may have actually seen an AI system blush.

I went down to the Aquacade where the swimming polars were just starting their matinee performance. Belinda had completed her signature opening dive and Otto the Elf followed her off the diving board tumbling and screaming all the way. The audience was eating it up. The Bearoness swam over to me with a quizzical look on her glamorous puss.

I leaned over and said, "The meeting went well. I'll tell you about it after the show." She smiled and dove back to join the precision swimmers as they made their intricate patterns with the occasional hiccup by Elfin Otto.

I ran into Dougal. "We're down to our short staff, Mr. Maury, but so far, so good. Oh, ye should know that Paul and Paula Polar have checked out and have just taken off in the afternoon shuttle helicopter to Abeardeen."

"Did they say anything, Dougal?"

"Just 'So Long and Thanks for all the Fish.'"

(Could that be the end of our Cranks?)

Chapter Twenty-One

A new character comes on the scene

He pops up on our Ursula's screen.

He is called Algernon.

Is he Dame Bearbi's son?

Were there two of them? What does it mean?

The evening performance of the Aquabears went off without a snag and Christmas at Polar Paradise slowly morphed into Boxing Day. Dougal, Ms. Fairbearn and Mrs. McRadish were doing wonders operating with a vastly reduced staff. No further incidents with the Crank(s).

The pantomime was booked solid and the main theater had 'standing room only' signs up. Ian and the stage crew had checked out the scenery, props and backstage areas several times. The same musicians were on hand and Bearyl was doing triple duty as Momma Bear, Stage Director and rehearsing for her New Year's Eve performance. Octavius was delighted to get rid of his abbreviated Santa outfit. On the other hand, McTavish had to be strongly persuaded not to wear his Christmas gift astronaut getup on stage. I was once again in my Goldilocks costume with my tail prominently displayed. Chita, Lepi, Jake, the Wolves and Flying Tigers were back in their front row seats. I'm not sure where Otto was. He kept zapping around the house. Condo with an Ursula unit in his claws took up his position on the light tower.

Bruce stopped backstage and brought Octavius and me up to date on the law enforcement situation. Superintendent Wardlaw and Sergeant McRuff had gone to their respective homes for Boxing Day but were standing by for

130

any emergency call. Fetlock Holmes was still in the hotel but was not attending the "panto." Bruce had a seat in the middle of the house.

Once again, the "too hot" porridge flowed; the bears went for a stroll; I tra-la-ed and skipped up to the house, went in and sampled the porridge; I sat and broke the chair and headed upstairs to find a bed that fit. Somehow, when I had entered the Bears' house, I had shut and jammed the front door. The returning bears couldn't get the door open and Octavius had to break it down. The audience thought it was part of the act and roared their approval. I told you pantomimes were supposed to be silly. Anyway, I was discovered, and I ran off screaming through the broken door into the forest pursued by all the bears. Curtain, applause, bows and Octavius held up the broken door to milk out a few last laughs. Later, I explained to all and sundry that the door was not a "Crank Prank" but just dopey me.

With the "Fearsome Feline" demonstration to Preston and the departure of Paul and Paula, we began to believe that the Crank problem had solved itself. With the arrest of the Terriers, those two Polars probably decided to leave town before it got too hot for them as well. The Pipers could certainly implicate them in the North Sea Oil incidents, if they decided to talk.

Several days passed on our way to year's-end and no further incidents surfaced. The full staff had returned and there was a small exodus of guests who had stayed for the Christmas celebrations but were going elsewhere for New Year's. They were replaced by an equal number of new arrivals who were looking forward to the vocal performances of Bearnice and Lepi as well as Chita, Jake and Bearyl at our New Year's Eve Gala.

December 30: Ursula set off her chime and asked to speak to me in private. Strange, but Ursula is strange.

"Maury, I must admit I am confused." *(Wow!)* I am faced with a case of duplicate identities. As you know, I have been vetting the current, outgoing and incoming guests looking for any potential threats or violent history. I've also included previous Castle residents like the Bearents Sea Bruins, the late Honoria Heifer, the piper Terriers and Dame Bearbi Da Savile-Row.

You, no doubt, remember Dame Bearbi's son Clarence, who killed Bearon Byron Bruin and attempted to murder the Bearoness at the Edinbeargh Opera House. He was arrested along with Dame Bearbi and condemned to life imprisonment. I just checked. He is still in confinement but during my Deep Data analysis of current guests in Polar Paradise, a polar bear with all the external characteristics of Clarence, showed up on my screen. He's been here several weeks."

"As far as I can tell, Dame Bearbi had only one son. This polar, named Algernon Maritimus Ursine, comes from Canada. I haven't been able to get a DNA sample, but the similarity is more than striking. Clarence lost part of his left front paw, resulting from a shot by Colonel Where at the Opera House. This bear's appendages are all intact but otherwise, he and Clarence are almost identical."

I was shaken out of my lethargy. "Great work, Ursula. Keep a constant vigil on this Algernon. I want to talk to Octavius, Belinda, Bruce and the Wolves. It may only be a coincidence but you and I both doubt it. Stay in the conversation."

I called them all together. Otto and Condo tagged along. When everyone was seated in the Lauren Bearcall conference room, I asked Ursula to repeat what she had told me. Once again, Octavius was all for taking immediate steps, but cooler heads were prevailing. Non-threatening Otto was elected to track down this Algernon, observe what he could and report back later in the day. Finding Algernon proved more difficult than we first assumed. On the surface, he looked like any number of other Polars. The resemblance to Clarence was in the details <u>AND</u> Ursula reminded Otto of the split right front paw print they found at several of the Crank attack scenes.

It was lunch time and the Otter decided to try a little impromptu entertainment in the dining room. By now, he was generally recognized as the resident clown. He had started out his adult life trying to be a magician. He was an abysmal failure till Imperius Drake got his talons into him, and unintentionally changed him into a teleporting illusionist by altering his genes. *(See Book Two – The Case of the Spotted Band)* He had demonstrated that talent this week with the Aquabears. Now he was going to fall back on his initial show biz efforts - Magic.

He zapped onto a small podium wearing a turban and holding a deck of cards. "Hello, everyone. Don't let me interrupt your lunch." A smattering of applause and laughter as the diners began to recognize him. "I thought I would add to your general boredom by performing a few tricks and reading a few paw palms. Do I have any volunteers?"

Two juvenile polars rushed to the podium. "Thank you, my young friends. Let's start with you, dear. Pick a card, any card. Don't show it to me. Now put it back in the deck. Good. Now, I'll shuffle the deck. Just one moment! Aah! Here is your card – the three of hearts. Is that right? Yes? (Applause) Now you, good sir! Pick a card. Whoops!"

He dropped the deck and the male polar picked them up. "Wait a second, Otto. They're all three of hearts!"

"I know. It makes the trick a lot easier." (Boos!)

133

"Oh well!" He zapped to the back of the room and appeared in an empty chair next to a bejeweled dowager. She screamed and dropped her fork. "Sorry, you looked lonely. Would you like me to read your paw palm?"

"No, I would not. Go away!"

He disappeared and promptly showed up on the opposite end of the room next to a mature male Polar. "How about you, Sir? May I have your name?

"Algernon!"

"Algernon, a noble appellation. Are you enjoying your stay at Polar Paradise?

"Oh yes! I've been having a lot of fun."

"Well, I hope you enjoy our New Year's Eve celebration."

"HaHa! I'm sure I will! I hope you do."

"Thank you. May I read your paw? Oh, dear, you have a scar on your pad. That makes it impossible to find your future line. Shall I try your left paw."

Algernon coughed, shook his head and said, "No, don't bother. I think I know my future."

"Gee, That's great. Very few of us do. Anyway, thanks for putting up with me. And thanks to all of you. Have a great holiday! So long!" He zapped and ended up out in the lobby.

"Are you locked onto him, Ursula?"

"Yes, Otto. I'm tracking him. Did you catch the irony in his answers to your questions? I think he's one of our Cranks. He wasn't alone, though. There may have been five or six of them altogether, if you threw in the now departed Pipers and Paul and Paula. Not exactly sure what their motivation was. I don't think it's all tied into the oil rigs. It could be something else."

"I agree. Algernon may be doing a solo now. I don't think he's going anywhere soon. The afternoon shuttle has already left. Let's gather the clan and strategize."

Back to the Lauren Bearcall conference room. Our team had regrouped. Otto and Ursula gave their information and opinion on Algernon. The consensus was to track him and wait to see who he's working with, if anybody.

Chapter Twenty-Two

Yes, December is practically gone

New Year's Eve will be coming anon.

With the musical show

And the dropping ball's glow,

All our guests will be carrying on.

December 31 early afternoon: There are two big New Year's Eve affairs scheduled – The Concert and the Midnight Drop of the Ball from the parapet. Plenty of opportunity for the Crank(s) to act up.

Super Wardlaw is scheduled to attend both events. We asked him to bring several of his "Finest" along with him and keep a police helicopter handy. Fetlock Holmes was also on the campus and we had our full complement of Octavian crime fighters at the ready. Lots of questions. Maybe we'll finally get a few answers.

Down in the theater and up on the front parapet feverish preparations were in progress. An 18-piece orchestra and 3 back-up singers had been flown in from Abeardeen, under the direction of Max Donald. He been hired as conductor and arranger by the Bearoness to work with Bearnice and Lepi on their grand tour and he was turning them into the polished professionals they now were.

Their repertoire for the evening was an eclectic mix of Scottish Favorites such as Annie Laurie and My Heart is in the Highlands; their comedy standards-The Indian Love Howl and The Lumberjack Song; and a selection of Christmas and New Year's traditionals, ending with a sing-along of Auld Lang Syne.

Lepi, also an accomplished keyboardist, did double duty and joined Chita on electric guitar and Jake on drums for a screaming and streaming rock interlude.

Between the two musical acts, Bearyl would present several of her stage monologues built around the turning of the seasons and the passing of years. All told, a true extravaganza presented by that consummate show biz legend, Bearoness Belinda Béarnaise Bruin Bear (nee Black) to say nothing of their stalwart agent, Mauritius Meerkat.

The stage had been set simply and mood changes were going to be carried off primarily by a complex sequence of lighting effects. At several times at past events, accidental or deliberately broken light towers, faulty rigging and assorted lamp failures had caused near misses for several members of our team. Needless to say, the lamps, lasers, housings, trunnions and clamps were getting a thorough going over and tests were kept under strict control. Condo, Otto and the Wolves, all capable of rapid movement, were assigned lighting protection duty. There would be no repeat of the Christmas Tree collapse.

Up on the parapet, the glass ball that would light up and move downward during the year-end countdown, was being run through a series of trials by the technicians hired to produce the effect. The Flying Tigers had that protection duty. The ball would slowly descend to the drawbridge and burst out in an array of colors announcing, "Happy New Year." The evening promised to be windy and special care was being taken to keep the ball from ending up in the moat.

Belinda was anywhere and everywhere. Mlle Woof had her paws full keeping the Cubs *(Pardon me…Astronauts)* from getting into everything and every place. Arabella, who was now stage struck from her "panto" performance wanted to know why she and McTavish couldn't be part of the acts. Pouts Galore! Octavius was having a long discussion with Fetlock Holmes and Bruce Wallaroo about crimes and criminals.

Tuning up; testing sound and lights; checking costumes; rehearsing the "lumberjacks;" practicing curtain calls and all other kinds of theatrical stuff took up the afternoon and early evening. Curtain at Eight.

Inside the hotel, a late lunch was winding down. Dinner would be served after the concert and would be a sumptuous buffet lubricated by an array of champagnes, liqueurs and other beverages. Then, as midnight approached, the guests would be led out into the courtyard to drink, sing, shout, cheer and watch the New Year's Ball descend. A small combo would play holiday music in the background. Dougal, Mrs. McRadish and Ms. Fairbearn were monitoring and managing in fine Scottish fashion.

Ursula and I were scanning the landscape while keeping tabs on our friend Algernon. He was participating in the revelry but in a rather reserved way. Nothing suspicious…yet!

Chapter Twenty-Three

The musical show's a big hit

But the Castle's abruptly unlit.

Is this one last prank

From our most recent Crank?

TNo, there's more if you'll wait just a bit.

Seven-thirty and the Theater was filling up with a noisy crowd of guests who had started celebrating early. The usual mixups on seating. Small groups of sows gossiping in the aisles. A couple of juveniles sprinting up and down. Drs. Chiti BingBang and Odd Vark had brought several of the Clinic patients down for the show and for the dropping ball later.

Our team had taken up their assigned posts and were watching and waiting. Belinda was seated in a box with the Cubs, Mlle Woof and Superintendent Wardlaw's mate, Lassie. Octavius was standing in the back of the house. Off to one side, Fetlock Holmes was in conversation with two large dogs who were obviously members of law enforcement.

Exactly at eight o'clock, the house lights dimmed, the orchestra struck up an overture I couldn't identify, and we were off and running. The curtain opened and out strode Bearnice and Lepi. Bearnice opulently bejeweled and Lepi in his glorious pelt and luxurious tail made a glamorous study in contrasts. They opened with an up-tempo song and segued into the Scottish airs to thunderous applause. They had the audience eating out of their paws.

After a few more numbers, the curtains opened further to reveal Chita and Jake. Bearnice headed backstage to change her costume and Lepi strode over to a keyboard set up next to a pair of mikes. Jake's drum set flashed in the lights and a burst of lasers accented his opening beats. Chita howled, the back-up singers crooned, and the atmosphere changed. Once more the audience was on their feet clapping to Jake's and Lepi's rhythm while Chita opened up with her Stratocaster guitar. She and Lepi sang a rock medley. Then to everyone's surprise, Bearnice reappeared in a new costume and joined the jamming felines, roaring to the beat. Bedlam!

Belinda was beaming, the Cubs were in ecstasy and even Mlle Woof was hopping about. Jake finished off with an amazing drum solo, lights and lasers flashed and Act One came to a crashing conclusion.

The audience headed out to the lobby bars and rest rooms and lots of discussion during the twenty-minute intermission. *(Interval, for you Brits.)* Chimes rang out summoning them back to their seats. The lights slowly dimmed, and the humming of voices deadened. The curtain parted, and a single spotlight shone down on Bearyl, holding an antique book in her paw. For the next twenty minutes, she captured the audience with an emotional rainbow of poetry, musings, dramatic readings and reflections on the passage of time and the changes of age. As she finished, the house was silent and then, a standing ovation.

The orchestra struck up a familiar theme - The Lumberjack Song. Lepi, wearing a plaid shirt and backed up by eight hearty bears, began his lyric "I'm a lumberjack and I'm OK." He got no further when all the lights on and off stage went out. Only the exit signs were still on. Questions, followed by mumbling, followed by incipient panic. The entire castle went dark.

Security personnel carrying flashlights started leading the audience out of the theater into darkened corridors. Battery powered emergency lights lit up large sections of the floor. Down on the utility deck, large generators snapped into action and soon Polar Paradise was back in business.

Octavius said to no one in particular, "What just happened?"

Dougal was on the line with the power technician. "Someone threw a master breaker. We don't know who. It'll take a few minutes to switch back from the generators. Ye can carry on with the show."

Most of the audience who had not wandered far in the darkness started to reclaim their seats. The curtain was closed to allow the players to regroup. The orchestra began walk-in music. There was a momentary outage as the generators switched off, but then power resumed.

Belinda was outraged. "That was no accident. I thought when we arrested the Pipers and the stunt double polars took off, we had seen the last of the Crank Pranks. Where is this Algernon? Is he a Prankster?"

Otto and I had the same question. We went out into the hall where we were joined by Belinda, Octavius and the Wolves. Ursula was on the line.

"Where is Algernon?"

The AI system responded. "I don't know. When I switched to battery backup and rebooted, I lost him. I'm scanning now. He's not in the theater or the utility deck. He may be outside."

Meanwhile, the show resumed and Lepi once again told the hearty bear chorus that he was a lumberjack and definitely OK. Bearnice emerged and fluttering her false eyelashes, sighed for the hunky Leopard. Then, of course, things disintegrated rapidly as the song came to its ridiculous conclusion. She

141

rushed from the stage weeping and the hearty bear chorus, disgusted, abandoned the puzzled Lepi. Long laughs and applause.

The performance ran its course, finishing with a massive singalong of Auld Lang Syne. Because of the power delay, it was eleven-forty-five when the crowd left the theater and formed up in the frigid courtyard to watch the dropping ball. Dougal, Mrs. McRadish and Ms. Fairbearn were standing off to the side. A musical combo was playing holiday songs; the security staff was on high alert and spread out over the area; Superintendent Wardlaw and his sergeants were moving about. Frau Schuylkill and Colonel Where each carried a weapon.

A podium had been set up at the foot of the drawbridge. Belinda and Octavius could address the crowd and watch the falling sphere at the same time. Mlle Woof and Chita had taken the Cubs in paw and held them away from the podium, in case there was a repeat of the falling Christmas tree. The glass ball, ten feet in diameter, was swung out over the edge of the parapet.

Just as it began its drop, a large figure wearing a cloak and mask jumped aboard holding on to the support cable. The crowd had started to count down but fell into stunned silence. The figure roared and shouted "Happy New Year, Bearoness. This will be your last." As the ball approached the drawbridge, he pulled a shotgun from beneath his flowing cloak and fired at the podium. The pellets missed Belinda, shattered the podium and hit Octavius in his front paw. Colonel Where fired three shots at the whirling phantom, hitting him in both arms. He lost his grip on the cable, fell on the drawbridge roof and tumbled into the moat. Over the cries and shouts, a screaming female voice could be heard, sobbing and howling. "Algernon. Oh God, Algernon! Save my boy. Save my boy! The voice belonged to Phoebe Fairbearn.

Epilogue

It's time to wrap up our long tail.

Listen now to Ms. Fairbearn's travail.

It's a story so sad,

And we're sorry to add

Her son Algernon's going to gaol.

Two members of security jumped into the moat and pulled the unconscious polar out of the water, laying him first on the drawbridge platform. Doctor BingBang took charge while Doctor Vark saw to Octavius' wounds. Two of the Shetland Police took hold of Phoebe Fairbearn who continued to sob but didn't resist. Superintendent Wardlaw had security set up a cordon around the moat and under Doctor BingBang's direction moved Algernon's body off the drawbridge so the crowd could return to the hotel. "He's alive," said the Orangutan to the Superintendent, "Broken up a bit but he'll survive. We'll need to extract the bullets he took from the Colonel's weapon and set a couple of cracked ribs. We can give him emergency treatment at the Clinic. You can set up a guard and then transfer him down to Abeardeen gaol. I'd like Doctor Vark to look at him, too. Clearly deranged."

Octavius had two shotgun pellets in the flesh of his left paw. No broken bones. Doctor Vark led him up to the Clinic where they could remove the shots. "You'll hurt for a while but with the exception of small scars, no permanent damage."

Meanwhile Bruce Wallaroo, Fetlock Holmes, the Wolves and I took Phoebe into a conference room. After checking on the shocked Cubs and assuring them that Poppa would be all right, Belinda joined us. Chita came along. Ursula was also on duty. "All right," said the Bearoness, "We asked

143

you this before. Just who are you? A straight answer would be greatly appreciated."

Before she could answer, Chita blurted "Omigod, You're Bearbi's sister, aren't you?"

The Housekeeper nodded her head. Belinda looked shocked. I made a remark to Ursula. "Can you check this out?"

"I'm on it."

"First of all, my real maiden name is Phyllis Phelps. Much to my regret, I am married to Jack DeLad. Bearbi and her pretensions to the aristocracy were all a smokescreen. She is Bearbi Phelps, but she wanted to impress your former husband, Bearon Byron Bruin. So, she made up a phony title and set off after him. She succeeded to the point of becoming his mistress and he kept seeing her even after he married you. He used to smuggle her into the castle."

"Then she became pregnant and had two male cubs. Byron said he'd support one cub but not two and to pick one and kill off the other. Your husband was a real swine. Bearbi wouldn't do it. I was living in Canada at the time and she persuaded me to take Algernon. Her magazines were doing well, and she provided me with extra money which I sorely needed. Algernon found out that I was not his mother and wanted to get back at Bearbi and the Bearon, even though he loved me."

"He persuaded me to move to England and we took up life in Liverpool. I was a housekeeper for a society family and Algernon went to work as a newspaper reporter. That's how he found out more about Bearbi and Clarence. He suspected that Clarence had killed the Bearon in that avalanche. Before he could get to Bearbi, she and Clarence were arrested for attempting to murder you, Bearoness. He started to fixate on you, saying that you were responsible for his being deserted by his wealthy father. I couldn't persuade him otherwise."

"When I stupidly married Jack DeLad, Algernon had a falling out with him and disappeared. Now I know he was plotting to ruin your life the way he thought you had ruined his. The next time I saw him was here at the Castle almost a month ago. He was posing as a reporter covering your holiday festivities. He told me about his plans of harassment and ultimately, killing you off. I couldn't bring myself to turn him in and I thought if I helped him with some of his pranks, I could talk him out of his crazy plans. Obviously, I was wrong. I'm truly sorry, Bearoness and I guess I'm guilty of aiding and abetting but he is like my very own son."

Fetlock Holmes stepped out of the room and called Superintendent Wardlaw. The Bearded Collie entered the room with one of his sergeants and took Phoebe out to the police helicopter.

Belinda shook her head. "I don't know whether I should laugh or cry. Bruce, Fetlock, I want to help her. Can you use your influence on law enforcement to go easy on her?"

"We'll try, Bel. It looks like you had several different Cranks. I hope we've seen the last of all of them. I guess Preston Pavel Polar wasn't one of them. Neither was Brittany."

"I hope so, too, Bruce. I think I'm going to spend the holidays next year on a desert island with Tavi and the Cubs. Chita, you can run the festivities. After all, you're a partner, too."

The cat looked cross-eyed at Belinda and they both broke out laughing.

"So, Bearoness, now that the excitement is dying down and Polar Paradise will be emptying out, what do we do for an encore?"

"I don't know, Maury. Tell you what. Why don't we make a movie?"

The End of
Volume Eight Of the
Casebooks of Octavius Bear

The Crank Case

About the Author

Harry DeMaio is a ***nom de plume*** of Harry B. DeMaio, successful author of several books on Information Security and Business Networks as well as the eight-volume ***Casebooks of Octavius Bear.*** A retired business executive, consultant, information security specialist, former pilot and graduate school adjunct professor, he whiles away his time traveling and writing preposterous articles and stories.

He has appeared on many radio and TV shows and is an accomplished, frequent public speaker.

Former New York City natives, he and his extremely patient and helpful wife, Virginia, and their Bichon Frisé, Woof, live in Cincinnati (and several other parallel universes.) They have two sons, living in Scottsdale, Arizona and Cortlandt Manor, New York, both of whom are quite successful and quite normal, thus putting the lie to the theory that insanity is hereditary.

His e-mail is hdemaio@zoomtown.com

You can also find him on Facebook.

His website is www.octaviusbearslair.com

His books are available on Amazon, Barnes and Noble, directly from MX Publishing and at other fine bookstores.

Also from MX Publishing

MX Publishing is the world's largest specialist Sherlock Holmes publisher, with over two hundred titles and one hundred authors creating the latest in Sherlock Holmes fiction and non-fiction.

From traditional short stories and novels to travel guides and quiz books, MX Publishing cater for all Holmes fans.

The collection includes leading titles such as Benedict Cumberbatch In Transition and The Norwood Author which won the 2011 Howlett Award (Sherlock Holmes Book of the Year).

MX Publishing also has one of the largest communities of Holmes fans on Facebook with regular contributions from dozens of authors.

www.mxpublishing.com

Also from MX Publishing

The Missing Authors Series

Sherlock Holmes and The Adventure of The Grinning Cat
Sherlock Holmes and The Nautilus Adventure
Sherlock Holmes and The Round Table Adventure

"Joseph Svec, III is brilliant in entwining two endearing and enduring classics of literature, blending the factual with the fantastical; the playful with the pensive; and the mischievous with the mysterious. We shall, all of us young and old, benefit with a cup of tea, a tranquil afternoon, and a copy of Sherlock Holmes, The Adventure of the Grinning Cat."
Amador County Holmes Hounds Sherlockian Society

www.mxpublishing.com

Also from MX Publishing

The Detective and The Woman Series

The Detective and The Woman
The Detective, The Woman and The Winking Tree
The Detective, The Woman and The Silent Hive

"The book is entertaining, puzzling and a lot of fun. I believe the author has hit on the only type of long-term relationship possible for Sherlock Holmes and Irene Adler. The details of the narrative only add force to the romantic defects we expect in both of them and their growth and development are truly marvelous to watch. This is not a love story. Instead, it is a coming-of-age tale starring two of our favorite characters."
Philip K Jones

www.mxpublishing.com